LONE MOUNTAIN
MELISSA SMITH

Copyright © 2025 by Melissa Smith

All rights reserved.

No part of this publication may be reproduced, distributed, or transmitted in any form or by any means, including photocopying, recording, or other electronic or mechanical methods, without the prior written permission of the publisher, except as permitted by U.S. copyright law. For permission requests, contact [include publisher/author contact info].

The story, all names, characters, and incidents portrayed in this production are fictitious. No identification with actual persons (living or deceased), places, buildings, and products is intended or should be inferred.

Book Cover by Elizabeth MacKenney – Berry Graphics

More by Melissa

By Melissa Smith:

WHAT I DIDN'T DO

A Bar Harbor Psychological Thriller

THREE SPLIT SECONDS

A Camden Maine Psychological Thriller

Melissa also writes Erotic Romance under the pen name MEL S.

DEMON ESHA TRILOGY:

Demon Esha

Becoming Esha

Desiring Esha

EMBER:

THE ENTICING BACK STORY OF RACHEL'S MOTHER.

RACHEL

THE TRILOGY CONTINUES!

Dedication

I'd like to dedicate this book to my dad.
I'm proud to be a farmer's daughter.
Thank you for raising me on Lone Mountain.
I love you.

Contents

1. Chapter 1 — 1
2. Chapter 2 — 10
3. Chapter 3 — 19
4. Chapter 4 — 26
5. Chapter 5 — 37
6. Chapter 6 — 47
7. Chapter 7 — 56
8. Chapter 8 — 63
9. Chapter 9 — 73
10. Chapter 10 — 86
11. Chapter 11 — 97
12. Chapter 12 — 107
13. Chapter 13 — 121

14. Chapter 14	130
15. Chapter 15	137
16. Chapter 16	145
17. Chapter 17	154
18. Chapter 18	165

Chapter 1

Forty years goes by unbelievably fast. It seems that in the blink of an eye, you're met with the gut-wrenching feeling that your life, your memories, your story, even your very existence has been nothing but a dream. Most people are but a blip on each other's radars. Like ships in the night, we pass each other silently, with little to no thought of connection. We are lost in our own worlds, caught up in the day-to-day grind, spinning in incessant circles for fear that if we stop spinning, everything will stop. In reality, stopping is the most glorious part of living.

These were my thoughts as I sat on my back deck, awaiting the first full solar eclipse in sixty-five years. This was a real once-in-a-lifetime occurrence. I was deep in retrospective thought. My daughter was scheduled to graduate high school in a couple of months. Truth be told, I'd been deep in thought about many things lately, all revolving around nature's biggest magic trick: time.

When I was a little girl, I would awake every morning to the gentle humming lull of the milk pump across the road at our fourth-generation dairy farm. The noise, while irritating when waking me, became a sound I desperately missed in my life. The years have flown by, and I still crave the sounds of that farm. From the tractor engine to the mooing of impatient animals to the quiet noise of the rippling brook where I fished, I still find I miss those days more than I ever imagined I would.

Properties tease us. They tempt us and lead us to make choices that we otherwise wouldn't make if nostalgia would stay at bay. But nostalgia never stays at bay and when my family farm appeared in the real estate guide one morning, I knew my life would never be the same.

Andover, Maine is a tiny town in the western Maine mountains. Green, grassy fields and rolling hills covered in wildflowers are perfectly backdropped by mountains filled with pine, spruce, oak, and maple trees. Hundreds of years of old-fashioned tradition are baked into the landscape, entrusted from generation to generation. This little piece of heaven was suffocating when I was a teenager. Now, as I start my fourth decade of living, I appreciate the simple beauties in life. A peaceful day of solitude in spring, watching life reawaken from the slumber of the cold winter months, a walk along the riverbank with your best friend, a night counting stars... Those are the things that matter. Those are the memories that are cherished forever.

***

I turned left off SR 5 and pulled into the driveway of my family farm. I couldn't begin to ballpark a figure for how many times I'd driven in and out of this half-moon driveway. I instinctively swerved around bumps and holes that no longer existed.

Even with my windows rolled up I could smell cows, diesel, and hay. I could hear the tractor rumbling in the distance and I could see my grandfather walking back to the house, his shoulders slumped under his blue coveralls. I blinked a tear away and when I did, he disappeared. I parked in front of the garage and sighed deeply before opening the door and stepping out into the morning air. It still smelled of cows, diesel, and hay, and I smiled.

"Hello, Miss..." A man with thick-rimmed glasses stretched his hand out to me.

"Amelia," I replied.

"Nice to meet you, Amelia." He shook my hand tepidly. "Let's walk this way. I'll give you the grand tour!" He started walking toward the house.

"Actually," I called after him. "If you don't mind, I'd like to walk around by myself for a bit. I'll meet you back here in twenty minutes."

I did not wait for his approval. I walked around my car, locking it as I went, and made my way up the small incline to the right of the red garage. The grass was bent over, thick, heavy with the weight of the last remnants of winter. When I was a child, this was a beaten path. It was a trail leading from the barn to the garage; a fun place to chase my sisters when we were little.

I walked toward the old barn. It was clean, sadly. A clean barn is an unused barn, but that is what has led me to this moment.

As a Pisces, I've always been a dreamer. As a farmer's daughter, I learned at a young age the importance of hard work. I learned to watch the way the world works. I learned all about the cycles of life, money, and the importance of integrity and planning. I started setting money aside with my very first paycheck. Money for something. Money for someday. I knew in my gut that someday was now and something was this farm. I had built up a solid business plan, a map if you will, of what I wanted to accomplish by purchasing this property. I wanted to create a haven, a destination for people who needed a chance to stop.

I walked through the barn, the secrets of my past lingering in my brain as I strolled by long alleys of free stalls. I stopped and smiled to myself as I recalled riding on the bucket tractor with my dad as he cleaned out the sopping, stinking, runny manure. It dripped down the bucket, and I struggled not to pinch my nose closed. I wiped a tear away at the memory and continued walking until I found myself at the base of a steep hill on the backside of the barn. I looked up the hill. I could picture it covered in white snow, perfect snow for sledding. I shook my head to clear the memory and kept walking until I was at the edge of a field. I looked out over the olive landscape. The bright green colors of summer had not yet awakened under the old leaves and branches, a testament to the harsh winter months.

I turned around so I could take in the entire farm. The barn and outbuildings were to my left and center, followed by the crimson-red garage where my grandfather could most always be found tinkering on something. Next to the garage was the garden, or at least that's where the garden used to be. The large white farmhouse was on the other side of the garden. It was surrounded by more fields that were eagerly awaiting warmer weather.

Fields that would be full of rich hay come August. When I was a child, I would ice skate on the small pond that would form in the center dip of the field. The wind would whip here, causing snow drifts to cross the street in winter. To my far right was yet another sliding hill. This one was longer and less steep than the bank behind the barn. We had many sledding parties in the backfield when I was young, sliding and ice skating with my sisters while my parents cooked hot dogs over an open fire. I would never have imagined fields and hills could create so many memories in my mind, but they had. The best memories were being towed behind my dad's old snow machine. We spent hours and hours playing in these fields. Tag, hide and seek with our friends, even manhunt in the dark of night. These fields, these hills, they housed my heart.

I walked back toward my car, past the outbuildings that once held shavings and grain, past the pen that used to contain rambunctious steers. I stopped instinctively to search for the wire fence that blocked off the yard and garden, but there was no fence. There was no garden now either, but I still couldn't bring myself to walk through the spot where it used to be, so I walked around. I walked past the old chicken coop and shed to the back steps of the farmhouse where the realtor was waiting for me.

"Any thoughts so far?" The man asked, stretching up to his tiptoes, presumably so he'd be taller than me.

"I'll take it," I chirped.

"Fantastic!" The man smiled ear to ear. "Do you want to see the house or..."

"Nope, I'm good," I answered his question before he could finish asking it.

"And you know about the house across the street and all that entails?" He tried to stop the grimace from clouding his expression but failed.

"It's fine." I pulled my sunglasses down to make unrestricted eye contact with him. I handed him my card with all my contact info on it. "You'll make the arrangements?" I asked cooly.

"Yes ma'am," he smiled. "I'll be in touch."

"I want to close in two weeks. Fourteen days," I stipulated. "Can you make that happen?"

"I think that can be arranged," he nodded.

"Perfect, talk to you soon."

I walked briskly back to my car, leaving the short man standing there looking rather astonished.

Chapter 2

The house across the street from the farm was, at one point, the most beautiful home in Andover. A log cabin, constructed by a master craftsman, it was hard to look away from. It had a beautiful wrap-around deck, ensuring one could sit for hours. You could watch the sun rise and set from the porch. It had been my mother's favorite part of the house.

The main level was quite massive, complete with a chef's kitchen, a large dining room, and an even larger family room. The middle level of the three-story log home was smaller than the first, enclosing four bedrooms and two baths. The top floor was smaller still, giving the house a sort of pyramid look. The home was an original design, unlike anything else in the area. When I was a young girl, I would go up to the top floor and gaze out the windows at the river flowing behind the fields. It felt magical to me, whimsical even. The house had sat empty now for who knows how long. The earth threatened to swallow it whole. Vines and overgrown rosebushes entangled the porch and clung to the old logs for dear life. The driveway had been blocked off with fallen trees. I sat at the end of the farm's driveway and stared at the decrepit cabin.

"The first thing I'll do is stain you back to your original color," I whispered to the hollow house.

I knew it wasn't the house or the stain's fault. Time was the cruel culprit, as always. The years tinted the wood a dark ash color. It was fitting. Part of me wanted to tear the old house down, but I knew that wouldn't scrub away the memories that had rooted themselves deep in my soul.

***

When I arrived home later that evening, my daughter Chloe had prepared dinner for us. Chloe turned eighteen in December. She was my little Christmas miracle, that's what I always said. I hadn't mentioned the Andover property to her. I was sure she was voting for a condo in Myrtle Beach rather than a farm in the middle of nowhere. As she went on and on about her day, I decided now was not the best time to tell her.

I lay in bed that night and stared at my dark ceiling, my entire body filled with wonder. I was more than ready for this move. Chloe would be away at college soon. She was already packing her bags to head west. California held possibility and promise for Chloe. I was excited, watching her chase her dreams, and I knew it was my time to chase mine, too.

Chloe was strong-willed from the day she was born, and I taught her to be independent on purpose. I taught her, and she taught me. Together, she and I were a force to be reckoned with. I was grateful for the timing of my new purchase because I would need a distraction after she left for college. This project couldn't come at a better time. Once she saw my plans for the place, she would forget all about Myrtle Beach.

I am a career restauranteur: a Jill of all trades. I started out washing dishes and cooking burgers like most teenagers did in Andover. Restaurants, convenience stores, and babysitting are the only real options for youth work, especially if you don't have a driver's license or car and can't travel out of town. I've always loved cooking. My mother showed me how to cook at a very young age and I connected with it. I would even dress up like a waitress and take my family's dinner orders on Saturday nights. I should have known then that my life would be one of hospitality.

Chloe and I live in a second-story walk-up in Portland. An exciting city full of growth, Portland offers a unique perspective for anyone in search of something different. Portland can be brutal, like anywhere, but it's also arty and seductive. The food scene is off the charts incredible. It's what had brought us to settle here in our quaint one-bedroom apartment where I slept in the living room and honestly didn't mind. The money I saved by only having a one-bedroom rent was well worth any discomfort or lack of privacy. Chloe and I have lived here for ten years, almost eleven. I am the head chef at a fine Italian restaurant in the heart of the Old Port. For most of my career, I was a server. That's how I managed to put away enough money for the down payment for the farm. Each slight slap of my ass, each disgusting dirty wink, and each spilled cup of coffee were all worth it now.

I'd drawn up my business proposal and retained the required financial estimates months earlier when I heard the property might be going on the market. I'd drawn out every last detail, right down to costs spent on carnival prizes and hayrides each Halloween. I made it impossible for the bank to turn down my request. In fact, by the time I finished pitching my ideas, they wanted to invest. April in Maine can be a dreary time. The cold can cut through your bones, mostly because it's April and you are not prepared. You want it to be summer, but summer isn't ready yet. This April was especially chilly. Perhaps it was the weather, but I dare say it was more because life was about to drastically change. No one talks of the subtle self-destruction that comes naturally with motherhood. Maybe I'm original; perhaps this anguish is mine alone, or could it be that no one dares speak of such things? I wasn't sure. All I knew was that I'd lost myself in Chloe. She'd become my world far quicker than I could have imagined. Motherhood had come easily to me. The PTA meetings and playground councils, the bake sales and sleepovers and crustless sandwiches; it was all such a joy to be Chloe's mother. What was I now? Now that her bags were packed and her heart set on a destination far from me.

I knew this day would happen a long time ago. At the age of seven, Chloe became fascinated with all things California. Her heart was there, her body urgently trying to catch up with it, and who could blame her? California was alluring, beautiful, and dangerous. I'd once dreamt of going there myself, a long time ago when my favorite television show was CHIPS, and it wasn't the handsome police officers that caught my eye. It was the sparkling ocean waters and the long, long stretches of steaming highway. Highway that would surely transport you to the life of your dreams. Now, that was Chloe's dream, and I wished nothing but success and happiness for her future. In some senses, I felt like I was being given a second chance at living; a second chance to put my dreams first. I certainly hadn't done that when I was young. Now I'd been given a new lease on life. I was scared to death, but also beyond excited.

If I'm going to be honest, with Chloe graduating, I feel like I'm losing a part of my soul, a part of my very essence. I feel like I'm not a mom anymore, even though I know that's not true. New things will come our way, for Chloe and me, and I'm excited to experience those chapters. I just can't shake the feeling that I'm being selfish. Shouldn't I follow her to California? Am I being irresponsible in staying behind? Not that I was invited to go... Yet my soul wanders. I have needs unmet and dreams undreamt. I have my own life to live still; I'm more than just a mom, and that humbling thought is mesmerizing to me.

I have big, big plans for the Andover property. The little town is resistant of change, and I keep that knowledge tucked away in the back of my mind. It just means I have to try harder and jump higher to complete my goals. I want to transform the old farm into a working, breathing, overnight retreat. A spot for people who want a hands-on experience, where they can enjoy tours of the fully operational dairy farm, snatch their eggs from the chicken coop, and then sit down to a farm-fresh, home-cooked breakfast. A place for weddings, group events, horse-drawn sleigh rides, and even tastings in our very own distillery. It will be paradise. Each room in the charming six-bedroom farmhouse will warmly await guests. The property could be booked by a single party, or each guestroom can be reserved independently. The property will have groomed trails for ATVs on the back acres, a tasteful mini golf course in the bottom field, and private glamping sites across the road near the river. I had so many dreams that I could barely remember them all. A full spa, complete with steam room and massages. Private chef tastings, cooking classes, and our own maple syrup factory. We would have pigs, chickens, goats, cows and, of course, horses for trail rides. I'd already connected with the local horse association to discuss possible collaboration. Working together with my neighbors would be key to making this venture successful.

I was extremely excited about the farmer's market space I wanted to create. It would be a place for artists, growers, and bakers to showcase their goods. The prospect gave me goosebumps. Andover was home to countless crafters, woodworkers, painters, masons, chefs, gardeners, photographers, and more. There would be a spot for everyone. I hoped to foster an environment of inclusion rather than competition. There would be plenty of competition on the mini golf course!

Chapter 3

I suppose I should tell you a bit about my past, my life. It's not super interesting. I'm a quick study. I grew up in Andover, Maine, the middle daughter of a multi-generational dairy farmer. My parents were regular people, high school sweethearts, most likely to get married, the couple everyone hated to like but had to. They were sweet, down-to-earth, lovely people. While I know my dad always wanted a son, he was blessed with three girls. After my baby sister was born, they never had any more children. Maybe they would have if they'd been given more time. But, as I said in the beginning, time is nature's biggest trick.

I was ten, my older sister fifteen, and my younger sister four on the last day I saw them alive. Those memories are so crisp, even now, thirty years later. My older sister Alice was dressed in frayed, stonewashed jean shorts and a light pink top that she'd cut and tied together in the center just above her belly button. Sometimes, I sit and wonder what might have happened if Dad had been home that day instead of haying. If he'd seen Alice dressed like Hoochie-Mama-Barbie, he never would have let her leave. But my mother had no control over Alice. She never had. As far back as I could remember, Alice never got in trouble. She could throw the craziest temper tantrums, saying and doing things I never dared do, and my mother would never raise her voice at her. I think that's why she blamed herself. It's what ended her life early, too.

Jenny, my baby sister, was wearing a flowery summer dress. Her little strapped sandals were a pale yellow color. I'd watched Jenny climb into the backseat of Alice's boyfriend's car. I didn't think much of it, because, at the same time, Alice started screaming at my mother, who was trying her best to get her to stay home.

"We don't like that boy!" she pleaded. "He's trouble..."

"I'm going!" Alice shouted.

"You're not!" My mom attempted to put her foot down, blocking the door.

Alice reached past her for her boyfriend's hand and the sweet taste of freedom. He yanked her out the open doorway, causing my poor mother to stumble and fall. She lay on the kitchen floor, sobbing. Alice and her boyfriend didn't look back as they drove swiftly down the driveway, with my little sister tucked away in the back seat of the rusty Oldsmobile.

I didn't know Alice's boyfriend. Alice was five years older than me. Our friend circles were entirely different. Alice and her friends were snobby and rude to me and my friends. The typical family squabbles ensued, and that's usually when my dad would bring me to the barn with him. He could tell the animals were good for me. And I was a good helper, even at a young age. The barn was in my blood way more than Alice's.

My mother was still sobbing on the kitchen floor when we heard the crash. It sounded like worlds colliding. The screeching and crunching of metal, followed by blood-curdling screams. The screams were loud; so loud, and I realized they were coming from my mom. She knew before she even saw anything. Even in her intense anguish, she protected me from the scene. The farmhands all ran toward the crash that was just out of sight from our house. The long stretch of road slithered around the bend and all I could see was smoke.

"William! William!" I heard my mother's screaming form into a name and soon William stood in front of us on the porch. William was twenty. He worked for us during the summer months when he was on break from college. He wasn't much to look at, scrawny. I remember thinking that even at the young age of ten. This was his second summer with us. He stood before us now, trembling.

"Yes, ma'am?" He struggled to keep his hands still.

"Stay here," she demanded. "Stay here with her. Do you understand me?"

I was surprised at the confidence and command in her voice as tears cascaded down her face.

"Ma'am, you shouldn't go..." William started to object.

My mother took my hand and pressed it firmly into his. She started walking down the middle of the road. I remember watching her walk. She put one foot in front of the other in such a direct manner, hesitant, yet steady. Calmly. Eerily calmly. I stood in the grass of our large yard and watched her go. The grass swallowed my sneakers. The hayfields were being cut now. Our yard could wait. Truthfully, it's what Alice and my mother had been fighting about. Alice was supposed to mow the lawn, but she'd refused, being headstrong and love-struck.

Alexander Brown had just turned nineteen. A high school dropout, he'd snagged my big sister's heart last year, when he still saw school as a priority. I'm sure it was the bad boy image that sucked her in. It gets all of us at least once.

Firetrucks and ambulances arrived on the scene, but not before my mother did. Maybe I should have held on to her for thirty more seconds. Would that have made a difference? If I clung to her and refused to let her walk away...

I saw my father's truck barreling through the hayfield, dust sifting through the air behind him. He parked in the far-left corner of the field across the street from our house, jumping out of the truck before it even stopped completely. Strange, how thirty years ago can feel like just yesterday. William sat with me in the grass until darkness blanketed us. Hours passed as we sat there watching the horrific death of my sisters.

I was never told details of the accident, but I heard things. I read things. I knew Alice had been killed on impact. The logging truck crashed into her side of the car. I knew Jenny had been thrown from the back window and died on the scene. I knew Xander was never seen again, dead or alive. I knew the logger was not at fault.

I never saw my mother again after that day. My father told me she was sick. I learned years later that she'd killed herself in a mental institution. I didn't blame her. I can't imagine what it must feel like to lose not one, but two daughters at once. I'd lost two sisters and a mother, but I'm sure my pain paled in comparison.

That night, I moved into the farmhouse across the street and my grandparents raised me, for the most part. My dad tried his best to overcome it, but he simply couldn't look at me. He became lost in drugs and alcohol and overdosed shortly thereafter. It was a predictable situation. He'd lost most of his world too, after all. I lived with my grandparents until I turned eighteen and then moved to Portland for college. The tragedy literally ripped my family apart. As an adult, it was years before I could even think of going back to Andover, back to where everything came unglued. Now, I find myself daydreaming of my return. Perhaps time does heal. I had concerns, of course, but I wasn't the same girl who'd left over twenty years ago. I was angry then. Scared, sad, lost. Now I had a purpose and a daughter of my own. I had gone on with my life. I had been the only one who had.

Chapter 4

"Mom, are you sure you'll be alright without me?" Chloe asked as she packed her last box of college supplies and dorm room decorations.

"I will miss you terribly. I won't lie," I assured her. "But I'll be fine!"

Chloe placed her hands on my shoulders and stood with her forehead resting against mine. It was something we'd done since she was a child, like our heads gave each other superpowers.

"Actually, Chloe..." I broke the silence. "Why don't you sit for a minute?"

"Okay..." She sat on her bed, looking nervous about whatever I was going to tell her.

"I'm going to be fine because I have a new project," I started.

"Oh Mom, not another man, please..." she interrupted me.

"It's not a man!" I stomped my foot. "And I take offense to that!"

"You can't. Your track record is horrible." She rolled her eyes.

"It's not a man, I promise. I bought some property."

"Oh?" I'd piqued her interest.

"Now, initially you might think this is crazy..." I started to warn her.

"Oh, I love it when you start things like that," she smiled. "Let me guess, you bought a condo in Myrtle Beach, like you've always talked about?"

"I did not." I shook my head. "I bought my old family farm."

"In Andover?" She asked.

"That's the one." I took a deep breath.

"I know, Mom," she grinned.

"What do you mean, you know?" I raised one eyebrow.

"I saw your notes on the kitchen table. Your business proposal and request for financing. You're not very stealthy."

"Why didn't you say anything?" I tried not to tear up.

"I figured you would tell me when you're ready. You must be ready?" Her eyes twinkled the same way mine did when I was excited.

"I am! I got approval from the bank, and I met with the realtor. I closed on the property a few weeks ago. I'm sorry I didn't tell you sooner," I apologized.

"Mom, it's amazing! Don't be sorry!" Chloe hugged me tightly.

"It's just... This time is supposed to be about you. I'm so proud of you, Chloe!" I could barely fight the tears now.

"It can be about both of us. I'm proud of you too, Mom! Your proposal sounded incredible. You've earned this! And I'll come home on breaks and help you. I can't wait to see what you build there!" She encouraged me.

"Thanks, honey!" I wiped my wet face. "I'm sorry it's not Myrtle Beach."

"Too many sharks down there anyway," she shrugged.

***

As I lay in bed that night, I thought about how much therapy I probably should have had by now. 'No use crying over spilled perfume...' The Pam Tillis lyrics hummed softly next to my pillow. The past was the past. I knew there was no changing it. Nothing could bring back Alice, or Jenny, or my parents, but maybe if I tried, I could make it so they were never forgotten.

"Do you think people would want to go there? You know, after what happened? Do you think it's too morbid?" I asked Chloe her opinion the next morning.

"I think it will depend on how you go about it. The vibe will be super important," she answered between bites of toast covered in Nutella.

Oh, Chloe. My adorable little Capricorn. Well, I guess she wasn't so little anymore. Graduation was upon us.

"I'll help as much as possible." Chloe put her hand on my arm.

"From California?" I asked skeptically, willing myself not to make her feel bad about her big move. I have a hard time controlling my body language nowadays. It was a skill I'd lost when I turned forty; a chain unbuckled.

"We can Facetime! You can show me everything!" She squeezed my arm. "In fact, why don't you show me the place before I leave? Tomorrow! We can do it tomorrow!"

"Really? What about your friends? Don't you have plans?"

"I'm making plans with you." She stood up and wrapped her arms around me.

"No, no, no! You hang out with your friends. I'm fine! I'm excited!" I assured her.

"Let's bring Claire and Johnny with us. They'll love it!"

Chloe immediately grabbed her phone and told her friends the new plan. I stood there speechlessly happy. I'd raised an amazing daughter, and I'd done it all alone. Sometimes, just looking at Chloe made me feel strong.

"I'll pack a picnic lunch." I smiled at my daughter.

I'd taken the week off from work for Chloe's graduation. There were many things to do. Bags to pack, marching to practice, ceremonies to attend. Goodbyes to be said. Chloe was driving to California first thing Saturday morning. The ground she walked on was on fire, smoldering with ambitions. She could not stay still.

The next morning, we picked up Chloe's friends and headed north. Shortly after we got off the interstate in Gray, my phone rang. It was the high school, wondering if Chloe was going on her class trip to Bar Harbor.

"Chloe Francis Brackley! You didn't tell me you were skipping your senior class trip today! Are you guys ok with skipping? Did you tell your parents?" I questioned the car full of stubborn, sneaky seniors.

"Mrs. Brackley, it's fine..."

"Please, call me Amelia," I suggested.

"It's fine!" They all said in unison.

"Alright..." I let my voice trail off.

We drove along SR 26, the radio blaring to the tunes of Macie Gray and Jewel. Chloe and her friends made me feel young again, appreciating the nineties classics I grew up with. It takes about an hour and a half to get from Portland to Andover, and it feels like worlds apart. Time magically stands still in Andover; life slows down. I spent so much of my childhood feeling angry; angry that my carefree, laughter-filled days were cut short so drastically, so unexpectedly, so fast. I was only ten years old when my family was demolished. Something like that forever changes a person. It molds you.

My grandparents tried, but they couldn't replace my parents. My mother was kind. She was compassionate and patient. She never angered. My sisters and I could resemble a wild tornado, and my mother would never raise her voice. Her sweet voice, that I so longed to hear again. Sometimes I thought Chloe sounded like her. My grandmother thought the best way to show her love was to keep me busy doing chores. I never had free time to wander off or sit and think. My teenage years were a tumultuous time for me. I longed to leave, especially after my father died, but I knew I had nowhere to go and no way to get there.

In my junior year of high school, I finally took driver's education and got my license. It quickly became my ticket to freedom. My grandfather let me use his old blue GMC, and I got a job uptown at Dave's General Store, making pizzas, burgers, and ham Italians. It was my first job outside the farm that had become my prison. More than a few times, I'd envisioned bars around the entire property. Now, for the first time in three decades, I pulled my car into the driveway that had once welcomed my loving family. Instinctively, I drove past the first entrance and into the second. I parked next to the rock wall that my dad had built with his bare hands. The weeds had overtaken it, sprouting out in every direction, much like the rosebushes that grew up the front of the log cabin.

"You okay, Mrs. Brackley?" Johnny asked from the back seat of my stopped vehicle.

"Yes, yes, I am." I shook my head to clear it. "And please, call me Amelia." I smiled and unbuckled my seatbelt.

I'd never brought Chloe here until now. It wasn't a place I wanted to introduce her to. I remained in my seat after the three of them got out of the car. Though the trees had grown in, and the grass was uncut, I could see the murderous corner in the road up ahead. It was clear as day. Chloe came around and opened my door.

"Show us around, Mom!" she requested excitedly.

She reached down, grabbed my hand, and helped me out of the car. I smiled at her, knowing I wasn't alone. Not yet anyway.

"Well, this is where I grew up. This was my home. It, um…it looked a little better back in the day." I shook my head again.

"Nothing a little loving can't fix!" Chloe interlocked our arms, and we started up the three front steps to the rundown cabin. The screen door fell off its hinges when I opened it.

"Well, there," I snickered, trying not to seem apprehensive to my daughter and her friends. "Maybe going in isn't the best of ideas," I sighed. "Who knows how safe it is?"

"Show us across the street. Show us the farm and your vision for it," Chloe encouraged.

I wondered if she could see through me. If my terrified ten-year-old was shining through. Thankfully, she spun around, her arm still interlocked in mine as she led the way to the street. As we walked, I could see myself and my sisters playing in the yard, riding our banana-seat bicycles, laughing carefree as we chased each other. I blinked, but the image wouldn't go away.

We crossed the street, and I stood quietly beside the old mailbox for a moment. The black box had seemed huge when I was a child. Now it was normal-sized, and the realization saddened me.

"Let's check out the hay barn first," I said, unwilling to give in to my mood.

CHAPTER 5

I led the way up the small hill to the old wooden hay barn. It was the only part of the barn that wasn't red. It left me wondering if they'd run out of paint or left it this way on purpose. Chloe and her friends passed me as they ran ahead into the barn. What was it about hay barns that made us revert to our inner child? My first instinct was always to run and jump into the first pile I saw. If they made a hay-scented candle, I would surely buy it! I followed the teenagers into the open barn. The massive door was rarely closed, except in the cold of winter, when it remained shut to keep as much warmth inside as possible. I bent down and picked up a handful of the scattered dried grass that covered the floor. As Chloe and her friends ran around the mostly empty room, I pressed the hay to my nose and inhaled. The scent made me smile as memories flowed freely through my mind. Memories of feeding my favorite cow, Six. Of holding her hay in my hands and scratching the white patch on her black head. Of talking to her for hours, this cow who probably couldn't understand a word I was saying.

"Excuse me!" A man's gruff voice called out, snapping me back to reality. "This is private property!"

"This is *my* property," I countered.

"And who might you be?" He stepped closer to me, away from the shadow of the large door so I could see his face.

"I'm Amelia Brackley, and you are?" I stepped even closer to him, refusing to give this man the impression that I was intimidated.

"Amelia?" The man barely whispered my name.

"Yes. I grew up here. I recently purchased this whole place." I waved my arms around.

"Wow, you're... you're all grown up." The man admired me.

"Mom, are you alright?" Chloe was at my side now.

"Yes, honey, this is..." I waited for his name.

"William," the man said. "I'm William."

"William!" I gasped, unable to hide the surprise from my voice.

"It's been a long time." He smiled slightly.

"Yes, thirty years since that day," I sighed.

William looked down at his boots.

"Thank you," I continued awkwardly. "Thank you for staying with me that day. I...um...I've wanted to say that for thirty years."

William tapped his cowboy hat at me but didn't say a word.

"So, you're still here?" I asked.

"I am. I live above the garage. I'm the caretaker," he replied.

"Caretaker?" I asked, confused.

"They didn't disclose any of this when you bought the place?" he asked, noticing my furrowed brow.

"You know, I'm sure it's mentioned in the paperwork somewhere and it's totally fine anyhow!" I laughed.

The last time I saw William was the day of the accident. He didn't come back to work after that, and I honestly never thought twice about him, other than wanting to say thank you. Now, thirty years later, he stood in front of me, a man, a full-grown, broad-chested man with a thick brown beard and tight Wrangler jeans. Chloe cleared her throat, and I squeezed her hand aggressively.

"Honey, this is William. I, um...I knew him when I was a kid. William, this is my daughter Chloe and these are her friends." I introduced everyone.

"Nice to meet you." William tapped his hat again. He started to walk away when Chloe hurried to stop him.

"Would you want to give us a tour?" I heard her ask. "It's been a while, and you seem to know the place well. We want to be safe, is all."

I rolled my eyes at my matchmaker daughter. William had his back to me, and I was all too happy to study his jeans.

"Only if you're not busy," I spoke up.

"Right this way." He held his arm out like he was directing traffic.

The five of us filed out of the old hay barn and followed William around the corner. At Chloe's discretion, she and her friends walked ahead of William and me.

"So, William, how are you?" I asked as we trudged along.

"I'm fine," he replied.

I got the impression William wasn't one for small talk. When we reached the far end of the long barn, Chloe stopped for directions.

"Let's head to the house." I pointed to the left and we continued our walk. "Over here is going to be the garden," I declared. "And out there, in the middle of the field, is going to be a mini golf course. There'll be a covered bridge over the pond and ice skating there in the winter."

"Excuse me, did you say mini golf?" William spoke up.

"Yes! It's going to be great!" I clapped my hands.

"This is a farm." I couldn't help but detect disgust in William's tone.

"This is a piece of land that was once a farm and will be again." I corrected him.

"With mini golf?" He raised an eyebrow at me.

"Yes, with mini golf. With mini golf and hayrides and farm-to-table food and apple picking!"

"It sounds amazing, Mom!" Chloe hugged me.

William glared at me over Chloe's shoulders, and I found it nearly impossible to look away from his piercing eyes.

"Go check out the house, honey." I handed her the keys. "I'll be there in a minute."

She ran off with her friends and I stood face to face with William, whose posture had changed dramatically since he heard the term 'mini golf'.

"Is there a problem, William?" I asked, resisting the urge to step closer to him.

"You'll ruin this place. You're going to commercialize it and ruin it," he scoffed.

"It's my place," I argued. "I can do what I want."

"We'll see about that." He turned on his heels and started to walk away.

"Why didn't you buy it yourself?" I hollered after him.

He spit on the ground.

I snickered.

"I would have turned it back into a working farm, not a playground." He sauntered toward me, looking like a dark funnel cloud about to twirl out of control.

"I'm still going to do that," I promised. "I'm not crazy. I have a plan. A great plan, with a realistic vision and financing."

William grunted.

"I could use your help," I admitted.

"Well, I stay with the property. That's stipulated clearly in the contract that you apparently didn't read."

"Perfect!" I smiled sweetly. "I look forward to getting to know you." Then I turned and went into the farmhouse.

I've always liked fire. Sometimes I like to burn things just so I can watch the smoke rolling in puffs up to the deep blue sky. Nighttime, daytime, it doesn't matter. Each holds its own alluring spark. I like to stare into the flames and watch whatever's burning disappear. For the longest time, I wanted to disappear. After losing my family at such a young age, I struggled with feelings of guilt more than anything else. Guilt because I should have told someone my little sister was in the car, and guilt because no matter how hard I tried, I couldn't change anything. Mostly, I had survivor's guilt. I'd survived and no one else had. Guilt ate me alive until my early twenties.

The first time I fell in love, I knew I'd been spared for a reason. Her name was Chloe. When I found out I was pregnant, all I wanted to do was call my mom. More than anything, I wanted to hear her soft, reassuring voice. I couldn't do that, but from that moment on, I knew I would never be alone again, and to me, that was the sweetest gift I'd ever been given. Chloe completed me. She comforted me before she was even born.

When I walked into the farmhouse, I was met with a persistent game of twenty questions and none of the questions were about the property we were standing on.

"Who is that man?" Chloe blurted out before I could close the door.

"Did this place come with a sexy cowboy? Go, Mrs. B!" her friends chirped in.

"He is someone I knew when I was ten," I explained.

"Is he going to be my new daddy?" Chloe laughed.

"Chloe Francis!" My mouth dropped open at her brass comment.

Suddenly, a window broke in the far corner of the dining room. The glass shattered into a spiderweb. The noise startled all four of us and we ducked for cover.

"What was that?" Chloe held onto my arm for dear life.

"I'm not sure." I took a deep breath.

I stood, expecting to see William on the other side of the shattered pane of glass. No one was there.

"You know, this place is old. It needs some loving for sure!" I smiled at Chloe and her friends. "Let me show you around." I tried my best to ignore the window as I led Chloe into the next room.

Chapter 6

"Maybe I should stay." Chloe voiced her concern on the ride home. "You have your work cut out for you, Mom."

"You are not staying. This is my project," I argued. "You are not putting your dreams on hold for me. No way."

"But what about the window?" My sweet daughter was genuinely worried.

"That was a freak thing," I laughed. "Yes, it was strange, but I'll be fine and if I'm not, I'll let you know."

"Well, I'm only a plane ride away if you need me," she smiled.

My big girl, I thought. So grown up.

Later that week, we got all dolled up for graduation. A friend had told me to video everything, but I couldn't take my attention off my beautiful daughter long enough to work my camera. I didn't want to miss even a single thing. One smile, one laugh, one teardrop. I sat in the auditorium, my eyes glued to Chloe, my heart full of pride as I watched her walk across the stage and accept her diploma. Pride for this daughter I never knew I wanted. Growing up, after having an active, vibrant family life one day and none the next, I swore never to have children. I didn't want the responsibility or the myriads of emotions that accompany parenthood. I didn't want to have to worry about anyone but myself. I often tell people Chloe saved my life. She taught me how to believe in love again, like I had when I was nine. Even though it had been just Chloe and me all these years, I wouldn't trade it for anything in this world, or the next.

The day after graduation, I helped Chloe pack her Rav4 and hugged her goodbye.

"I'll see you soon, baby!" I did my best to sniff back my tears.

"Maybe I'll see you first!" Chloe replied.

"I'm so proud of you!" I kissed her cheek. "Now, do your best, and don't forget to have fun!"

"Same to you, Mom! I love you!" She wiped a tear from the corner of her eye.

"I love you so much! Drive safe!"

I felt like I was in one of those insurance commercials where the parents say goodbye to the fledgling leaving the nest to go to college. Certainly, this wasn't my life. Certainly, Chloe couldn't be fully grown already and heading to the faraway West Coast. What was I to do now? I closed my eyes and all I could see was William's husky frame looming in front of me.

Perhaps what I did next might seem a bit hasty. After Chloe's car left my sight, I went inside, called my realtor, and proceeded to list my home on the market. The realtor told me to start packing, because I wouldn't have any trouble selling the place. The apartment, while a second-floor walk-up, would be my nest egg. A modest sum that was sure to provide me with peace of mind. I packed all week and, sure enough, on Tuesday of the following week, I received news that it had sold. I had to be out in thirty days. I knew I didn't need thirty days. I was ready now. The next day I drove to the charming, historical-looking, brick real estate office and went inside, gave them my keys, and started my long drive home.

I've always been an all-or-nothing sort of person. I have the unique distinction of knowing up close and personal how short life can be. Its unpredictability was torture when I was a teenager. Those crucial moments when a girl needs her mom; when she wants her sisters close, those moments tormented me, digging into my skin like a dull serrated knife, ripping and tearing and ripping some more. I was always alone during those moments. Now, I knew it had formed me into a better human. I knew I'd done better for my daughter. That's what mattered the most. Life here and now, not life gone by.

I packed my car full to the brim with my most valuable possessions. Pictures of Chloe, handmade treasures she'd crafted in grammar school, ceramic knick-knacks she'd hand-thrown in high school, and, of course, everything in my kitchen.

When you're tempted by all things culinary, your kitchen becomes your playground. Not only is it where you play and experiment, it's where you work. As with any job, you need the proper tools to perform the tasks at hand. Is it my fault that there are ten thousand different kitchen gadgets? No! It was one of the things I was most excited about in the new house. Both houses had fabulous kitchens with marble countertops, big drawers, solid cupboards, and large butcher block islands. The log cabin across the street had one thing that made it a bit superior: my memories. My good memories. All my memories after the accident were tainted; stained by the haze of death.

Where did I want to live? Either house would be more than sufficient for me. I liked the idea of living in my parent's house, at home. The idea blanketed me with comfort. However, that was not the plan. The plan was for me to fix up the dilapidated house and rent it in its entirety to large groups. It would be the perfect retreat. When I'd devised my business plan, I said I would live in the farmhouse. I wasn't as emotionally connected to the farmhouse. Plus, I wanted to be on the same side of the road as the farm, which would require constant attention. I hadn't realized there was an apartment above the garage. That had thrown a lovely little twist into my well-thought-out plan. Now, I craved a tour.

I shook my head to clear my muddled thoughts of William. I recognized the fact that I knew nothing about him. It surprised me he was still there, on the farm. It had been thirty years since the accident. Thirty years since he'd sat with me on my front porch, neither one of us speaking, just listening to the unwelcomed sounds of sirens and emergency personnel. He'd been my hero in that moment, sitting with me in my numbness. I couldn't help but wonder what he was like now. How long had he been living on the farm? Why was he still there? As far as I knew, the property had been abandoned for almost ten years. It showed, too. The farm itself had maintained an alright appearance. I hadn't returned to the area until I saw the listing in the paper. It was easier to stay away than to confront the reality of my guilty conscience. I killed Jenny with my silence that day. In turn, I'd killed my mother; her shock and sadness at losing both daughters so violently had been too much for her to bear. And I'd killed my father, his anguish far beyond repair. But that was all thirty years ago. Now, I would return and revive my home. I would make the place beautiful again. Perhaps I could even help hurting souls in the process, making the farm a haven for relaxation, a respite from the rest of the world.

Excitement fueled me as I instinctively pulled into the driveway of my old house. My new house, now. I turned my car off and stared at my reflection in the rearview mirror.

"You've got this, Amelia," I whispered.

I took a deep breath and opened my car door. I grabbed the lanyard of keys from my center console and started up the front steps. The door was locked, to my relief. I'd been a little concerned I'd find it otherwise, with stragglers living inside. Sometimes my imagination went wild. I opened the door, and it creaked loudly. I half expected it to fall off its hinges like the screen door had done, but it did not. A small, informal kitchen table greeted me like it had always done when I was a child. Sometimes it would be set with after-school snacks. Other times it was piled high with laundry, each of us girls with our stack that we'd be responsible for putting away neatly. Once in a while, on rainy days, my dad would sit at the table with his adding machine and checkbook, mumbling at the faintly printed numbers.

I closed my eyes now and could see the toppled-over chair lying on the kitchen floor, broken as a result of my sister's tantrum that fateful afternoon. When I opened my eyes, I could see all three chairs correctly positioned around the table, as well as the wooden bench my dad made after Jenny was born. My dad was a skilled craftsman. Though farming was his full-time job, his passion was building furniture. All of his pieces were exquisite. Bookshelves, stools, gun cabinets, bedframes, even hope chests for each of us girls. Surely, if the table were still here, the rest of his treasures must be sprinkled throughout the house as well. I ran my hand over the woodwork on the trim of the kitchen cupboards. I remember watching him build these countertops. I would watch him for hours as he created life out of lumber.

The kitchen, while dusty and dingy, was everything I remembered it being, only smaller. I knew it was because I'd grown, and again, the thought humbled me. I'd been allowed to grow. Life is precious.

I looked out the kitchen window to the hay barn across the street. For a brief moment, I could see my dad as he walked home after a long day's work. I blinked, and to my surprise, he was still there, walking down my driveway to the front steps. He clunked his boots loud on the steps to loosen any dirt, the same way he'd always done. I ran to the door to greet him like I had when I was a child. I flung the door open, but the bearded man standing in front of me was not my dad. It was William.

"Oh, it's you," I said, unable to hide my disappointment.

Chapter 7

"What are you doing in here?" William asked rather rudely.

"I'm...I'm looking," I stammered.

"Looking for what?" he inquired.

"You know what, William?" I cleared my throat, ready to defend my presence to this arrogant man. Instead, I continued softly. "I'm not looking for anything. I'm looking around. Just remembering."

I stepped back from the doorway, running my hands along the kitchen table as I retreated. William stepped inside.

"I'm glad you're here," I beamed. "You can walk through the place with me. I'm a little timid all by myself."

"Walk through?" He raised one eyebrow.

"I'm trying to decide which house I want to live in."

I swallowed hard. He was making me so nervous. I could feel my palms becoming sweaty.

"I see." He removed his cowboy hat. "Are those girls coming with you?"

"Girls?" I asked, confused. "Oh, you mean Chloe and her friends? No. That was my daughter. They are all away at college now. Well, at least Chloe is. She went to California."

"So, it's just you?"

I wasn't certain, but I thought I detected a slight softening of his dark eyes.

"Yup." I shifted about the kitchen, trying not to show my awkwardness. "It's just me. Both houses are so big. I'm trying to decide..." I let my voice trail off as he walked to the center of the kitchen. Now only the butcher block island stood between us.

"I don't like your plans for this place." He scowled at me.

"Why not?" I asked.

"This is Nirvana," he replied. "It doesn't need to become New York City."

"Again," I huffed. "You should have bought it..."

"I did," he snapped back. "I lost it to the bank over the winter." He hung his head, and I resisted the urge to feel bad for him.

"I'm sorry." I stood as tall as I could. "But now it's my turn. I've been saving my whole life to come back here. This is my home."

"But you left," he said through gritted teeth.

"Yes, I did," I acknowledged. "And now I'm back."

I stared at him, and he stared at me. I didn't know he'd owned the place. I couldn't tell what he was thinking. His dark eyes swirled with anger and intrigue. He put his hat back on and turned to leave.

"I think I'll live here," I called after him. "For now, I think we could use the street between us."

He didn't reply. I shut the door firmly behind him, locking it as I wished SR 5 was wider than it actually was.

***

I spent the next few days cleaning, unpacking, and organizing my new home. A sense of calm surrealness settled over me. It felt good to be back. I'd reacquainted myself with each room, claiming the master bedroom for myself. Its jacuzzi tub called out to me. My realtor had arranged for the lights and water to be turned back on before my arrival. I was happy. The only blip on my radar was William. I couldn't do anything about him. He'd have to get over it. The problem was that I needed William. I needed his help and handyman skills to accomplish my goals. Without him, I'd have to hire someone. He seemed like the logical choice. And yes, it helped that he was gorgeous. Tall, muscular, bearded. Check, check, check. I had to figure out a way to get along with him.

The following Monday, I ventured into downtown Andover. It's just under two miles from my spot nestled at the base of Lone Mountain, to town. I say 'town' loosely. It doesn't consist of much, especially compared to Portland. There's a general store, a post office, a town office, a library, a small diner, and a hardware store. It's classic, small-town America. The streets are paved, but the lines are faded. The 'Welcome to Andover' sign was situated at the edge of a rustic campground I'd never seen before. *What a fantastic place to camp,* I thought. I remember being young and having campouts on our lawn in the middle of August when it was far too sticky inside to sleep under the roof. We'd cook out on the grill, my mother burning everything black; nothing a slice or two of cheese couldn't fix. Thus began my addiction to all things dairy. The campground added a nice touch. It wasn't there when I was a child, and I smiled at the thought of progress in this small town.

My smile faded when I entered the town office. The air was stagnant, smelling of peppermint candy and paper. Everyone looked up from their desks when I entered. I cleared my throat and stepped up to the nearest cranky-looking clerk.

"Hello." I greeted her when she didn't greet me. "I recently moved here and need some information on my property, if possible."

When I told her the address, the other three clerks snapped their heads up in my direction.

"Oh, you sweet thing." The woman in the far back corner piped up, removing her glasses as she spoke.

"Did you already purchase the property?" the curly-haired clerk in front of me asked.

"Yes ma'am. I'm looking for the deed, tax records, things of that nature," I informed her.

"Oh dear, that place is...well... it's haunted." Another woman whispered her two cents.

"I'm not concerned with that." I smiled kindly at them. "I'd just like the records, please."

I turned and sat in one of the two folding gray chairs. The flyers on the half-wall in front of me were typical waiting room flyers. Domestic abuse hotline phone numbers, help-wanted ads, information on how to get your water tested, and when the next animal clinic was. Oh, and the list of pedophiles in the area. Things of that nature. I studied each flyer.

"Miss?" The clerk peeked over the counter at me. "I can make copies for you to take for five cents a page, or you can take the originals into the side room over there and look at whatever you'd like. Which would you prefer?"

"I'd like copies, please," I answered swiftly yet politely. I couldn't wait to get out of the stuffy office.

Ten long minutes later, she handed me a piece of paper.

"I need you to fill out this request for documents." The clerk was all business.

She laid a large manilla envelope on the countertop next to me. I filled out the paper, wrote her a check, took my files, and left. Once outside, I felt like I could breathe again, happy to be out of that stifling environment. I got home and sifted through the pages. I filed them in my new black filing cabinet, but not before noticing William's name on the previous owner's document.

"Shit," I grimaced. "He's telling the truth..."

CHAPTER 8

Later that week, as the sun dropped behind the mountain, I sat on my new porch swing and stared out toward the river. With the farm, my farm now, to my right, I felt centered for the first time in a very long time. I dare say for the first time ever. I sat on the porch swing until darkness and stars blanketed the world around me. Suddenly, I heard a noise other than frogs and the occasional car passing by. I heard the strumming of a guitar. I rocked and listened to the twangy rhythm. It lulled me to sleep alone on my new swing.

The next night, I sat on my swing, hoping to hear the music a second night in a row, and sure enough, after darkness fell, guitar notes sang out like birds in the treetops. This time, I was prepared. I had a plan. I went inside my house and returned wearing my flip-flops and carrying a bottle of wine. I took a deep breath and decided now was as good a time as any to make friends with William. Maybe he wouldn't be so grumpy if he got to know me. I decided to walk around the long side of the barn so I could come up to the back side of the garage. It sounded like he was playing guitar on the west-facing deck he'd built. I rounded the corner of the barn and sank into the overgrown bushes, attempting to spy. Like the true city girl I'd become, I didn't watch where I was stepping and set my flip-flop-covered foot down on a pile of old barbed wire.

"Ouch!" I screeched, falling backward on the uneven ground. My bottle of wine smashed on a nearby rock. The guitar stopped humming and in no time at all, William was at my side.

"Flip-flops do not belong on a farm, ma'am," he said after inspecting my ridiculous situation.

"Neither do assholes, yet here you are," I replied, barely audible.

How dare he say something like that to me? So demeaning! Could he not see I was bleeding? He untangled the wire from my foot and scooped me up into his arms. I made an honest attempt not to snuggle into his chest, but I couldn't help it. He carried me back to his apartment above the garage. As we walked in the side door of the old red building, I was a bit taken aback that the interior hadn't changed. Unfinished pine boards served as shelves along each wall, each one home to some sort of garage trinket that would surely be devastating if lost. Dirty, dusty glass jars housed bolts and screws and nails. Some of the glass jars were so dirty you couldn't see through them. No doubt my dad and grandfather knew what was in each one without looking.

William carried me up the stairs along the back wall, an area that used to house bicycles and little red wagons when I was a kid. William's apartment was nicer than I imagined. Loft style, it was all open space, but clean and tidy. He didn't have a ton of furniture, but it seemed fitting for him, at least what little I knew about him. He plopped me down on the counter next to the kitchen sink and hurried to move a few dirty dishes out of the way.

Without saying a word, he picked my leg up and swung me around, so my injured foot and ankle rested in the bottom of the metal sink. He turned the water on warm and began gently rinsing the blood away. At first, I grimaced at the pain, but all too soon, I was mesmerized by his touch and forgot all about my cuts. He massaged my skin, cleaning as he did so with an ointment he'd taken from the cupboard.

"Bag Balm fixes everything," he said in true farmer fashion. "When's the last time you had a tetanus shot?"

"Um, two years ago," I recalled. I was thankful my brain still worked.

"What were you doing out there in the dark?" He turned to me; his eyes darker than I remembered.

"I was bringing you a bottle of wine." I shrugged, looking down meekly.

"You were spying," he accused me.

"I was not!" I felt my defenses rising. Why was he so irritating?

"Oh yeah? Well, where's my wine?" He glared into me, not at me, and I wished I could disappear.

I sighed heavily. "It broke when I fell."

"Great, so I'll get to clean that up tomorrow." He rolled his eyes.

"What exactly is your problem?" I hissed at him.

He reached between my legs and opened the drawer directly under me. He grabbed a hand towel from the drawer and wrapped my foot in it, without saying another word. I berated myself, angry that I'd enjoyed his touch even for a second.

"You know what? I'm fine!"

I wriggled free from his hands and towel and jumped off the counter. My ankle and foot throbbed, and within seconds, my skin was covered in blood again.

"You're not fine."

William quickly picked me up and set me down on the counter. Again, he started rinsing my bloody foot, not nearly as gently as before.

"Sit still," he commanded.

My heartbeat rang loudly in my ears, matching the tightening of my stomach down below. I shivered.

"I said, sit still!" he seethed.

I did as I was told. He rinsed and dried my foot and ankle before reapplying the ointment and wrapping gauze and tape tightly around my wounds. Then, he carried me down the stairs and put me in the passenger side of his truck. He drove me across the street and carried me up the three steps to my house. He opened the door for me and set me down inside my kitchen. I turned to thank him, but he was already getting back in his truck.

"You have a great night too!" I mumbled under my breath.

Perhaps I shouldn't waste my time or energy on him. He clearly had demons of his own. There was no way this was my fault; no way he was this angry because of me.

"I'll show him!" I whispered.

I hobbled to my closet and found my box labeled 'boots'. Opening it, I pulled out my big, bulky snow boots and slipped them on my feet, careful of my wrapped one. I grabbed my broom and dustpan, as well as a flashlight and a trash bag. I'd clean up my mess, thank you very much! I limped across the street, keeping my flashlight off until I got to the scene of the accident, then I flicked the light on and began sweeping up the chunks of thick green glass. I was almost finished when I saw his light coming toward me.

"Do you have a brain in that pretty little head of yours?" he growled.

This time, I didn't respond. I refused to feed into his aggression as I kept sweeping, then knelt to sweep the pile of glass into my dustpan. I winced with pain when I stood up and William was at my side in an instant. For the second time, he scooped me up into his strong arms.

"Enough of this!" He said as he once again carried me to the garage like a broken doll.

"Put me down!" I hollered at him.

He did not listen. Once inside, he set me on a kitchen chair and untied my boots. He took them off; my bandages on my ankle were red with blood. He didn't say a word as he picked me up, put me on the counter, and again cleaned and bandaged my wounds. When he finished, he carried me to his couch.

"Sleep here tonight," he said. "I'll get you some blankets and a pillow."

"No. I'm going home." I tried to argue.

"You'll sleep here, and there will be no discussion about it. I can't trust you to take care of yourself," he declared.

He walked away before I could object and a few moments later he returned with a pillow and a quilt. The sight of the old patchwork quilt made time reverse thirty years. Back when I lived in the farmhouse, now only steps away. Back when I'd sit and stare out the living room windows; my deepest desire was to go home. SR 5 was the only thing standing between me and my home. Twenty-five feet of pavement that I was forbidden to cross. Ever. A lifetime of memories I was doomed to forget. Suddenly, I was irrationally angry.

"I'd like you to take me home, please."

I stood and started walking to the door, limping like an injured barn cat.

"Don't be ridiculous. Sleep here. Elevate your foot," he ordered.

"I'm going home," I said, reaching for the doorknob.

He blocked the door from opening and my anger grew roots.

"Get out of my way!" I seethed.

My eyes must have shot darts into his because he blinked ferociously and backed away from the exit.

"Stubborn, crazy woman!" I heard him utter under his breath as I hobbled away.

I was prepared to walk home. Nothing was going to stop me. A few minutes later, he hurried to catch up with me.

"Wait. Just wait!" he hollered. "Get in the truck. I'll drive you."

I paused only a moment. My foot throbbed; I hadn't stopped to put my boots on. The gravel driveway stung under my feet. I did as I was told and climbed into his truck. He drove me across the street and helped me out of the truck and into my house once again.

"Thank you..."

I turned to relay my appreciation, but again, I was too late. He was already walking away, and I wasn't following him. I sat down in my recliner and put my feet up.

"Stubborn, crazy woman," I scoffed. "At least I'm not an asshole!"

Chapter 9

Over the next few weeks, William and I stayed out of each other's way. I was beyond busy. I'd decided to jump headfirst into my new project, and I began tackling the ever-daunting task of cleaning out the farmhouse. The house hadn't been in our family name for ten-plus years, so I found it very odd that it still looked the same way it did when my grandparents had it; the way I remembered. The more time I spent there, the less I thought the place was haunted. I became positive that William broke the window that day when I was showing the property to Chloe and her friends. It seemed like something he would do to scare us away. The joke's on him; I don't scare easily.

I went through the house and tagged everything I wanted to keep. The furniture was all genuine wood, most of it handcrafted by my dad. He'd been making furniture since he was a boy. You could tell from the pieces adorning the upstairs bedrooms, which ones were his early works and which ones he'd mastered. Some of the dresser drawers didn't close quite right. Some of the legs were uneven. It was of no concern. They were still beautiful.

Each day, I seemed to have a scheduled meeting with someone. The town had been giving me a hard time with my necessary permits. I knew it wouldn't be easy, but I hadn't realized the level of salacious ignorance that I would have to deal with. Lost or missing paperwork seemed to be the go-to response for most discrepancies. The selectmen and planning boards continued to give me a million hoops to jump through, but I didn't mind. I'd come all this way; I could jump hoops with the best of them. State inspectors, plumbers, electricians, code enforcement officers, contractors: each day there was a steady stream of people in and out of the farmhouse. I stopped watching for William.

My favorite part each day was going home at night. I loved walking across the street, down into the ditch in the center of the lawn, and up the other side, the same way my dad used to. Soon, I'd created a lovely path, reminiscent of days gone by. Each day, I felt more and more grateful that I could be here, in my home, back on my family land. I felt insignificant in the big scheme of things. I knew my time here was minuscule compared to others who'd been here before me. I became awed by the previous generations. Those who'd constructed this beautiful farm from nothing to what it is now, all the highs and lows in between. Ever-changing, farmlands live and thrive in the hearts and minds of those who work the soil, tend the harvest, and care for the animals. Everything is a journey of adoration. Everything needs time to survive and prosper.

I knew I needed to smooth things over with William. The tension in the air was thick enough to carve. Not seeing him seemed to make it worse. I knew he was around. I noticed he'd been weed-whacking and picking up old fencing and other hazardous objects. It made me smile a bit, knowing it was his way of baby-proofing the property for me.

One afternoon, I sat on my porch and watched him working across the street. He'd backed his truck up to the top of the little hill between the barn and garage. He was throwing things into the back, shirtless, looking very fine on this hot summer day. The sun was beginning to fall in the sky. His silhouette danced in my line of vision. Soon, I was lost in my imagination as I wondered what William looked like naked. His arms, shoulders, and chest had felt firm and muscular when he'd carried me into his home that night. It was a moment I thought of quite often when I was alone.

I knew what I would do. I went into the house and found an empty box. I filled it with packing peanuts that I still had from moving. I grabbed a bottle of wine from my wine rack and packed it firmly in the middle of the box, carefully surrounding each side with the foam peanuts. I closed the box and brought it onto the porch, where I watched as William rounded his truck over with what appeared to be trash. I'd noticed he'd been making a pile of unused, mostly broken tools, rusty sheet metal, and old barbed wire. Perhaps he'd gotten lost in cleaning the same way I'd gotten lost in planning. He tied down the contents of his truck and turned left out of the farm. I waited until his truck was out of sight and then carried the box of wine across the street and left it in front of the side door of the garage. I turned to walk away but thought better of it and walked the package up the stairs to the landing of William's apartment. I deposited the box on his welcome mat and walked home unscathed. I sat back on my porch swing, wishing I had left a note, but I was sure he'd know who it was from.

Twenty minutes later, William returned, his truck bed empty. I got up and went into the house to refresh my sangria. Then I came back out and turned on my gas grill. I threw a few of my handmade cheddar onion burgers onto the flames, closed the lid, and sat down on my swing to watch the scenery across the street.

It was almost sunset now, near quitting time if there was such a thing on a farm. William disappeared into the garage and, sure enough, emerged a few minutes later. To my chagrin, he was carrying the box of wine.

"The wine is for you, dummy!" I hissed under my breath as he crossed the street and walked up to me.

"Ma'am," he said, tipping his cowboy hat. "I think this is for you." He set the box down on the top step and turned to leave.

"Actually..." I jumped off the swing. "That was for you. From me. It was supposed to be funny."

"Oh?" he said, one eyebrow raised in confusion.

"It's a thank-you, for the night you helped me. Twice. I know I should have said something before now, I just..."

"I don't drink wine," he stated gruffly and started walking away.

"Wait, William..." I called after him, frustration lacing my voice. "Please, stay a minute?" I threw up my arms.

He stood still in my driveway, resisting the urge to flee that was written all over his face.

"I'm grilling burgers. I have beer. Stay for dinner?" I practically begged.

"Ma'am," he started to object.

"Please," I implored. "I'm sorry for all the trouble I caused you that night. I really am. I'd like to get to know you."

He was quiet for a minute before he responded. "Let me run home and change. I'll be right back."

"Great!" I tried not to jump up and down in excitement.

I watched him walk away, and I wondered what he'd been doing with his life in the last twenty years. I'd lived a whole other life. I'd had a daughter and a career. What had he done? Why did he stay here all these years? He seemed so alone. Ten minutes later, William was sitting at my porch picnic table. We ate burgers and potato salad.

"This is delicious, ma'am." He licked his lips.

"Please, call me Amelia." I smiled at him.

He cracked open another beer. The first one had gone down in two sips. He'd brought a six-pack from his place when he'd come back after his super-fast shower. I sipped my second glass of Sangria, willing myself to remain sober.

"Just wait until this burger is from our grass-fed livestock! Then it will be amazing!" I exclaimed.

"I will say you've been making a lot of improvements." He tipped his head to me like he'd forgotten he'd taken his hat off.

"Thank you," I eagerly accepted his praise. "And thank you for all your clean-up efforts. It has not gone unnoticed."

William's half-smile faded, and I wondered what I'd said to irritate him.

"Do you think you're my boss?" he asked after clearing his throat. He sat a little taller in his seat.

"No, William, I'm just saying thank you. Everything looks nice." I tried not to become defensive.

"Just so we're clear, I'm employed by the estate, not you," he specified.

"I've read the paperwork; thank you." I failed at not being snippy.

"Thanks for dinner." William stood up.

"William, I just want us to get along!" I stood up as well.

"Not going to happen," he sneered.

"Why?" I stood toe to toe with him.

"Because you're a snobby, inconsiderate, entitled little brat. You come here after disappearing for all those years and all you want to do is exploit this place. Exploit its history. Exploit its pain."

"How dare you!" I poked his chest with my finger. "This place ruined my life! It erased my childhood! I couldn't wait to get out of here. Away from all the memories. Away from that haunted corner!" I pointed south to the street bend that claimed my sisters' lives. "I most certainly will not be exploiting anything! I want this place to help people, to offer healing and wholeness. You don't know anything about me or my mission for this place–my home–because you haven't bothered to ask. Who's the snobby, inconsiderate brat now? Entitled? Yes, I am entitled. I own this place! I bought it with money that I worked very hard to earn; thank you very much! This is my home. This is not a business venture or a half-thought-out experiment." I took a step closer to William, swallowed, and looked him straight in the eye. "That being said, I highly suggest you learn your place."

"My place?" he spattered.

"Yes. I am not your boss, but I am THE boss. I pay the bills. I have the final say over what goes on. I'm grateful for all you do, but you must respect that I own this property now. I can do with it whatever I please."

William was mute. I didn't know if anything I said registered in his mind or not. He stood in front of me, his eyes wild. I felt my palms become clammy.

"I want to work together." I smiled a shy smile and reached out to touch his arm. He jerked his body away, and I looked down in time to see a jagged scar across his forearm.

"Why did you come back here?" he asked. His voice sounded fragile for the first time.

"Why have you stayed?" I replied with a question of my own.

"I have my reasons." He looked down the road again to the corner that changed my life forever.

"So do I," I sighed. "And I must say, I was happy when I realized you were here. William, you probably saved my life that day, holding me steady on this very porch."

He blushed.

"Please, don't mention it. That day was... That's the one day of my whole life I wish I could do over." He sounded very far off like he was in a different world, different time, different place.

"Same..." I said, thinking of my little sister's frame hiding in the back of Alice's boyfriend's car.

I wanted to ask William if anyone had seen Xander since then, but I didn't want to know the answer. Some questions are best left unasked. A few moments of awkward silence led William to say goodnight and leave. I watched him walk away. So many questions swirled in my mind. The first of which: Where did he get that nasty scar on his arm?

After that night, William and I magically got along. Maybe he respected me more because I stood up to him. Maybe he had misunderstood me and my intentions. Either way, he was much more amicable after that night. I put a large whiteboard in the garage on the wall where I knew he'd see it every day. At the beginning of each week, I'd list my goals, and I'd check them off on the whiteboard once they were completed. The third week in, William made a list as well. It made me smile. It also helped me coordinate from there on out. Soon, the whiteboard was covered with lists for the hardware store, schedules, and even groceries. It became our form of communication.

A month into it, I figured it was safe to try dinner again. August is a hot, tiring month for farmers. Let's be honest, most months are, but in August there's so much to do and you race the sun the entire time. I wrote 'Supper at Amelia's—8 PM' on the whiteboard calendar for the second Saturday of the month. Nothing was ever mentioned about it, but I had faith that the smell of my bourbon ribeyes and garlic mashed potatoes would waft across the street, luring William to my house.

It worked. And I can't tell you how many times I've wondered how different my life might be if I'd only minded my own business that night.

CHAPTER 10

I saw William trudging across the street at a quarter 'til eight. He carried a bouquet of hand-picked wildflowers and a bottle of red wine. When he popped the cork and poured us each a glass, I could tell from his demeanor that he had lied before when he said he didn't drink wine. There were so many layers to William. I had the distinct feeling I had only just begun to scratch his surface.

"Thank you," I said. The strap of my slinky sundress slipped slightly off my shoulder as I spoke.

"Thank you," he replied. "For everything. This place is starting to look in tip-top shape!"

"Thanks to you!" I clinked my glass to his. "We make a pretty good team."

"I like the whiteboard," he complimented me.

"That's a trick I learned from my daughter," I explained. "Since Chloe was old enough to hold a marker, she loved whiteboards. For Christmas one year, I got her the whole fancy whiteboard set like you'd see in kindergarten with magnets for months, days, and even the weather. Amazingly, she's not going to college to be a weather forecaster." I caught myself diverging down the path of over-sharing about my daughter, who I so desperately missed. I quieted myself.

"You must miss her..." William observed more than asked. His husky voice was softer than I'd ever heard it.

"I do!" I sighed. "But I talk to her on Sundays and she's doing well out there in sunny California! How do you like your steak cooked?" I asked as I turned to the grill, grateful for the distraction so I wouldn't start crying. I always had to hold back my tears when I thought of Chloe. I knew she was happy, healthy, and flourishing out west, but I hadn't prepared myself for the level of loneliness I felt without her.

"Oh, medium-rare, I'm not too fussy." William walked to my porch swing and sat down.

"I've never met a cowboy who isn't fussy about his steak," I teased him.

"Wow, this swing is nice!" He smiled and nodded his head. "What a perfect view!"

I watched him as he swung and, for the first time, I saw a childish side of him. It warmed my heart.

Our meal was perfection, as I knew it would be. I didn't doubt my culinary skills. The only person I knew who cooked as well as me was the owner of the Little Red Hen Diner in town. Her food tasted like home every single time I ate there. I'd discovered the little gem one morning on one of my many pilgrimages to the dreaded town office. The owner was young, vibrant, and smart, and she paid extreme attention to detail; a quality that was highly sought after in the restaurant world. Truthfully, I wanted her to work for me. I was waiting for the right time to proposition her. I hadn't lived here very long yet, and I wanted to get to know people before I allowed them into my circle.

"Should I open another bottle?" I asked after William's wine disappeared rather fast.

"I don't see why not," he chuckled.

William had a sweet laugh. I'd become quite smitten with him over dinner. He was a completely different person when he wasn't being an uptight jerk. I was impressed and hopeful and praying he couldn't see the stars embedded in my eyes.

"I think your vision for this place is admirable," he admitted as we both started our third glass of wine.

"Thank you. I want there to be some good that happens here. You know?" I couldn't take my eyes away from the dreaded corner.

"I know." William shifted next to me on the porch swing. "Are you warm enough? I can start a fire."

"I don't have a fire pit." I waved my arm over the yard.

"Of course you do." He handed me his glass of wine and took off around the back side of the house, toward the small utility shed. A few minutes later, he returned with an old rusty wheel rim. He beamed with pride. "Where would you like it?"

It surprised me, he asked, instead of putting it wherever he thought was best.

"There is fine," I smiled.

I couldn't take my eyes off the piece of history he'd uncovered. I remembered that rim well. We used it as a fire pit back when I was a child. Hot summer nights were never complete without roasting marshmallows and eating s'mores. I watched while William dug a hole in the lawn to the left of the porch and nestled the heirloom firepit inside. Next, he went to the tree line and gathered twigs and branches for kindling. He placed his findings in the center of the pit and walked to the wood pile where he grabbed an armful of firewood. I felt like I was in a trance watching my dad build a fire, my sisters and I running around the yard catching fireflies.

"Hey, do you have a couple of camp chairs you want to set around it?"

William snatched me away from my memories. I looked down at him from my elevated position on the porch. I set our wine glasses on the small table next to the swing and took one step down to him as he took one step up to me; I couldn't help myself as I wrapped my arms around his neck.

"Thank you," I whispered. "I love it."

"Oh, well..." he squeezed me back slightly. "It's nothing. I can build it up for you too, with some rocks and stones. We can make it look nice."

I willed myself to let go of him and he turned back to tend to the fire while I went inside in search of chairs. A few minutes later, I returned with two chairs and a little camp table. I set them up around the blazing fire and put our wine glasses and s'more supplies on the table.

"You can't have a fire without s'mores," I stated the obvious.

Just then, a shooting star darted across the black sky, and I was indeed seven years old again. In this very place, at this very moment. I shivered.

"Let's get you a blanket."

William ran up onto the porch and snagged the blanket off the back of the swing. He wrapped it snuggly around my shoulders. I stared up into his dark eyes; the light from the fire danced gleefully in his pupils. He cleared his throat and sat down. An awkward silence threatened to engulf us.

"I can't believe some people live their whole lives never experiencing a night like this," I said as I sat down in my chair.

"I know," William agreed. "I could never be a city boy."

"Oh, it's not too bad!" I laughed. "Although I can't quite picture you in a suit and tie."

"Hey, I spiff up nicely! Thank you very much," he scoffed playfully.

We both took a long drink of wine.

"Damn," I said. "This wine is going down easy tonight."

"Yes, it is," he said, not taking his eyes from mine. "I should get going."

"What? No! We just started the fire," I objected all too quickly.

"You don't need me here to enjoy the fire."

He stood up and drank the rest of the wine in his glass before setting it back on the table.

"I don't think you can trust me by fire all alone," I whined. "Remember how clumsy I was around the barbed wire?"

"Oh, I remember!" He leaned down toward me, wagging his index finger at me like I was a naughty girl. "Thank you for a lovely evening." He touched my shoulder briefly while he wrapped the blanket tighter around me.

"You don't have to go," I said.

His scent drifted in the air around me. I eagerly breathed him in.

"I do." He cleared his throat uncomfortably.

"Why?" I asked, licking my lips and biting my bottom one.

He groaned coarsely. "Because I never should have come here in the first place."

I grabbed his sleeve and pulled him down to me.

"And why is that?" I inquired; my heart thumped wildly in my chest.

"Because I shouldn't do this." He shook his head slowly from side to side before leaning in to kiss my neck.

"Mmm," I moaned, my breathing coming rapidly now. "And why shouldn't you do this?"

"I just shouldn't," he whispered.

His wet mouth trailed a path from my neck to my chin and finally up to my lips, where my mouth met his with matching passion. I wasn't sure why he found it so taboo, but I didn't concern myself with it as I freed my hands from the warm blanket and wrapped my arms around William's hard, sculpted body. His shoulders were so defined, even through his shirt. The wine on his lips and tongue fueled me, igniting sweet feelings that I thought were lost forever. Yes, I'd had romances here and there, but this... this was passion unlike any other.

William gripped my waist and pulled me up into his frame. I wrapped my legs around him, and he carried me to the porch.

"Take me inside," I directed.

His biceps bulged under his shirt, and I wondered how the fabric didn't rip. He set me down on the kitchen table, my blanket long since disappeared. My dress threatened to fall off on one side.

"You're so beautiful," he proclaimed, his deep raspy voice melting in my ears.

He had his hands in my hair now, his lips clinging to mine as his robust tongue swirled in my mouth, wanting.

I pulled his shirt apart, breaking the snaps as I went. His chest was mostly smooth, with only a small hairy patch in the center. He was sweaty. His heart pounded, much like my own. I pushed his shirt down his shoulders, then one arm, and another. I paused, my hand tracing his right arm and shoulder. His rippled flesh, while healed, had been gashed and torn, the skin scarred.

"William." I pulled back from his kisses. "William, what happened to you?" I asked, my voice and eyes both pleading.

He blinked in front of me. Once, twice, before stepping back. He tugged his shirt back on, frustration evident in his movements.

"William, I'm sorry. I shouldn't pry..." I tried to apologize.

"It's not you. Thank you for dinner." He pressed a quick kiss to my cheek. "I just... I can't do this."

With that, he left. I sat paralyzed on my kitchen table. My mouth was sore from his touch. There's no way he wasn't into me; no way he didn't want me. So, what the hell happened? I took a deep breath, gathered my wits, and went in search of sweatpants and a sweatshirt. I dressed and went back outside to sit by the fire, desperately hoping the flames would shed some light on my peculiar situation.

Chapter 11

The next day I got up at sunrise, figuring I'd go to the Little Red Hen and catch the owner before her morning rush started.

"Wow, you're up early today!" She exclaimed when she saw me walk in.

"I am," I nodded. "I am in dire need of coffee and bacon."

"I have both!" She smiled at me.

I'd been here a handful of times since I arrived in this tiny town. Today, I was the first customer. Surprisingly, I beat the short, cranky old man who had been here every other time I'd been here. The man, while irritable at best, had wonderful stories which he told on repeat. Stories of when he was a guard for President Eisenhower. Stories of how he once spanked the president's grandson for tearing a page out of his logbook. Stories of all the crazy things he would find at his garbage truck job. Frozen boa constrictors, brand new shoes still in the box, and old artifacts he'd rescued and used to decorate his turn-of-the-century home. When I first met him and he introduced himself, I told him who I was. The next time I saw him, he produced an old book on the history of Andover, from which he showed me black and white pictures of Andover back in the day. Pictures of my family's land and homes, photos of my great-great-grandparents, as well as the grandparents I knew. Pictures of people I'd never heard of. He was a treasure, this man, and I'd hoped he'd be here this morning, but he was not.

"Hey, I have a question," I asked between sips of coffee.

"I may or may not know the answer," Mae replied.

"I purchased the farm on SR 5, about a mile before the covered bridge," I started.

"That's awesome!" Mae responded. "I've noticed a lot of work going on there. Congrats!"

"Thanks!" I smiled appreciatively. "I'm in the market for someone who wants to work with me in the kitchen, with potential for growth, and I don't mean to overstep, but you are my first pick."

"Oh, wow!" She held her hand over her heart, in awe. "That's such an honor! Thank you for thinking of me!"

"Of course! Your food is amazing!" I continued. "I admire your work ethic and organization. I aim to create a peaceful haven for people. Everything will be farm-to-table. There will be a farm stand and a fully operational dairy farm. I'm even putting in a mini golf course, although I'm getting push-back on that." I rolled my eyes.

"This town loves to push back! They slow progress as much as humanly possible." Mae's eye roll matched mine.

"Small towns are like that," I nodded. "I actually grew up here. I'm just finally coming back home."

"Welcome home!" she beamed.

"Thank you!" I couldn't help but like Mae. She seemed very real, which was hard to find nowadays. "Listen, I can see you have a great thing going here, but if you want to stop in sometime, check out my place, and see my vision, you'd be more than welcome. I'd love to collaborate with you in any way possible."

"I'll stop by. I'd love to see the place!" Mae replied.

"I look forward to it!"

I felt a bubble of hope well up inside of me. Maybe I'd have a new friend here, a real friend. I'd left all my friends in Portland. It's not too far from here, but far enough to make friendships falter a bit. I didn't have close friends to begin with. I've always been sort of a loner. It wasn't unheard of for me to go out alone, but honestly, I rarely ventured out. It's how I was able to purchase the farm to begin with.

***

Later that afternoon, I grabbed a blanket and a towel and headed to the river. In my mind, my dad went with me. He carried a tin pail of worms we'd dug together and our fishing poles. My hands were empty as I joyfully skipped along the cow path to our favorite fishing spot. This spot was perfect in August because just up the hill was a grand blackberry patch. Before Alice fell in love with Xander, the two of us would come here and pick berries for pie and cobbler. We always ate half of what we picked before we got home. Now, I gazed at the brook with all its twists and turns and dark places where you *knew* the trout were hiding but still never had any luck reeling one in. I walked along the bank to where it dumped into the Ellis River. The little stream quickly became big and wide as it entered the massive corner. The loop of the river created a natural sandbar, much sandier now than it was when I was a child. Sometimes on hot summer days, we'd pack a picnic and spend the day on the sandy beach. Not many days; there were always too many chores to be done on the farm, but occasionally on a sunny afternoon with little to no breeze, we'd venture down here. I sighed as I watched the water flowing downstream. Over the years, I've found the 'occasionalies' are what matter most. Occasionally, I'd go shopping with Chloe and her friends. I always felt like the third wheel when we started, but by the time the day was over, it was always a cherished memory. When she was four years old, we would have tea parties on the apartment floor once in a while. We would both dress up in my clunky boots and a fancy outfit. That didn't happen a lot, but occasionally. Those are the times I want back; those are the strings that have sewn our life together.

I laid my blanket on the grassy pasture, unsure of my commitment to go swimming. I'd come here to think. As I lay back on the blanket, I watched the green treetops swaying overhead. It wasn't windy. The branches were alive with activity as squirrels raced along them. Imagine being so uninhibited. Squirrels weren't scared of falling, of plummeting to their death below. They scattered from branch to branch without a care in the world. William was currently my care. Thoughts of him weighed me down, still. He'd been nothing short of a puzzle since I arrived here two short months ago. I could not figure him out. Was he simply shy? Did his scars embarrass him? It was obvious something traumatic happened to him. Something happened that he didn't want to talk about.

I knew my best bet was to forget about him romantically. He was a farmhand, nothing more. I knew my inquisitive nature would balk at such a thing, but I could try. I had plenty of things to keep me occupied besides William. My initial goal for opening had been Labor Day weekend. Fall in Maine is spectacular with its vivid colors. The crisp nights and sometimes still warm days are wonderful. It's perfect sleeping weather with your bedroom window open. I knew my goal was not achievable; I had way too much to do. I needed to hire more help, and I knew William would dislike the idea, so I hadn't brought it up. I had a compromise in my back pocket that I was holding on to, should I need one.

I'd made a ton of progress in two months. I knew from classic Maine politics that if you wanted community support, it was important to get on the good side of the locals. I knew I had to hire any help from within the confines of this tiny town. Thankfully, there were options everywhere. Local painters, electricians, carpenters, and plumbers, Andover was stacked with deserving options. I had crews working to repaint the white farmhouse and outbuildings, as well as carpenters who were refreshing the barns. The best painter, Ned, I'd reserved for the ever-important job of re-staining my log cabin. He'd stained it the first time, right after it was built. I remember watching him, mesmerized. He worked in smooth, steady strokes as the sun glistened off his tan body. Now, thirty years later, I wanted nothing more than to sit and watch him work, preferably with a margarita in hand. He hadn't changed much over the years. That was another thing about Andover; it, and its people, doesn't change. I had changed. I had gone out into the world and come home years later, certainly not the same girl who'd left.

I laid on my back under the brilliant blue sky and tried to think of a name for my new home. Something simple and classic, nothing fancy. I wanted something with meaning. Something strong. I'd thought about calling it 'Chloe's Place', or 'Amelia's', or 'Haven on the Ellis', but nothing stuck. Everything sounded foreign and wrong. I knew I should stop thinking about it and then I'd figure it out, but I had such a hard time doing that. I couldn't shut my mind off.

I lay on the blanket and thought back to when this pasture was loaded with cow patties; back to the days of my youth, when I'd won multiple trophies at the town fair for throwing cow dung the farthest in what was called the Cow Chip Flip. Most participants went about it the wrong way, the safe way. They threw the round mounds of dry shit like frisbees. Not I. I would dig to the bottom of the pile, find the moistest one, pack it into as firm a ball as possible, and chuck it with all my might. It was a fail-proof method. As I looked at the green grass around me, I was saddened by the lack of manure. Soon, I thought. Soon!

A little while later, as I walked up the hill to go home, my attention was captivated by Lone Mountain. The mountain nestled meekly behind the farm. It wasn't large like Mount Washington or vast like the mountains that made up Sunday River Ski Resort in the surrounding town of Newry. It was scenic and charming, comforting even, as it guarded our little slice of heaven. I knew the name of my place. I didn't need to think about it any longer. My retreat would be called Lone Mountain. Shivers cascaded up and down my spine and I knew it was perfect.

Ideas flooded me. There was so much I wanted to do here, so many possibilities! Paint 'n Sip nights, line dancing classes, fishing excursions, and even guided hunting expeditions where you could kill your own game and then learn how to dress and butcher the animal, whether it be a rabbit, pigeon, or deer. I wanted to foster a deep appreciation for this land, this place where I was lucky enough to grow up and call home. I knew it would be far too much work for just William and me. And I also knew I didn't need his approval or permission to hire anyone.

Chapter 12

Frugality is something that has always come second nature to me. I hate spending money, and I especially hate spending it on myself. I like my bank account to maintain a certain amount of digits. I'm the type of person who would rather do a job myself instead of paying someone else to do it, and I knew this venture would be challenging to me in that regard. I could not do everything myself; bare minimum, I needed William, and I wanted us to be on good terms. I needed to know I could count on him. I needed to know a lot more about him than I currently did, and I had no idea how to go about this daunting task. He intrigued me. He mystified me, really, in more ways than one. His avoidance game was top-notch. I never saw him, yet everything was always done and always above expectations. He must have worked at night or become a ghost.

One Monday in early September, Mae stopped in for a visit. I was in the garden beside the garage, tending to my raised beds of cucumbers and jalapenos. Harvest was fast approaching. Next year, I would double my veggies and hire a gardener. Cooking was my forte, not gardening. I didn't have a green thumb.

"Hey there!" Mae called out as she approached. "Wow! Look at all your beds! This is incredible!"

It wasn't incredible. It was, by far, a work in progress, but I accepted her warm compliment eagerly, eating it up like sweets to a child.

"Mae, hi! Thank you! What brings you by?" I cringed, sure that I sounded more skeptical than I meant to. I wasn't used to having friends here.

"I was wondering if you'd be free to chat. I know, I should have called. I saw you out here when I drove by."

She smiled at me, and I thought how lovely it would be to be near someone other than a contractor or a grumpy farmhand.

"No worries at all! Stop by anytime! It's great to see you!" I beamed, silently telling myself to chill out. "Most of the time, I feel like I'm on an island all alone here," I shrugged.

"Oh, I know the feeling! Trust me!" she commiserated.

"You want a tour? I'd love to show you around."

I removed my gardening gloves and straw hat. I always thought my grandfather looked silly in a straw hat. Now I understood the necessity of one. I'd found his old, tattered hat hanging on a nail in the garage. It was dirty and falling apart, but I claimed it immediately. It settled snuggly over my blond hair, nestling just above my ears, doing its best to block the sunshine from my brow.

"I'd love to see the place!" Mac nodded happily.

Over the next two hours, I abandoned my chores and took Mae building by building, explaining my vision for this glorious landmark. The chef's kitchen inside the farmhouse was almost completely refurbished and I couldn't wait to show it off. It was my favorite space. We walked to the farmhouse last, the spunk in my step undeniable. I had become happy here, among all the chaos, and it felt good. I felt like younger me, pre-tragedy, skipping along with my sisters to my grandparent's house.

The old farmhouse was a large ranch with a door in the center. A breezeway and porch were off the right-hand side. I was redoing the landscaping surrounding the front door, planting flowers, and placing pavers to create a beautiful pathway. The employee entrance was to be off the side porch, complete with a ramp for deliveries. I would store paper goods and catering equipment on the breezeway. I'd constructed wooden shelves with doors to hide any clutter. Everything would be labeled, neat, and organized. On the back of the breezeway was a screened-in sunroom, where employees could sit and have breaks, or I could plan menus while having the perfect view of the working farm. I wanted this place to be serene for everyone, not just my guests. I'd worked in enough establishments, so I knew the importance of having a great working environment. It was essential not only for morale but for quality of work.

The door off the breezeway entered into a short hallway. There was a full bath on the right, followed by an office. The old office still had my grandfather's roll-top desk in it. I kept it where it was; I was honored to be able to sit there and work now. The office also housed a washer and drier and utility sink. The room across from the office had been my grandparent's bedroom. I completely renovated it, insulated it, and built storage space. I transformed it into a walk-in, refrigerated room. It was state-of-the-art, complete with stand-up freezers on one wall. Mae's mouth dropped open when she walked in. It was immaculate. Chrome shelves lined two walls, while bins for produce were situated in the center under a stainless-steel table. On the last wall where the closet had been, I created a separate section for all things dairy.

"Amelia, this is dreamy!" Mae exclaimed.

"Thank you! I love it!" I couldn't help but beam like a kid on Christmas morning who'd gotten everything she ever wanted. "Let me show you the kitchen; it's my pride and joy!" I giggled, a noise I hadn't heard myself make for quite some time.

I took her by the hand and led her down the rest of the short hallway.

"Oh, Amelia!" Mae's eyes drank in every detail of my carefully crafted kitchen.

An extravagant, shiny Southbend range and flattop combo took up the right wall of the kitchen. There were four burners, along with wispy wavy grates, that gave it a somewhat magical appearance. To the right of the burners was a thirty-six-inch pristine flattop griddle. It patiently waited to sear farm-fresh eggs and fluffy pancakes. Two convection ovens lived under the stove and flattop. Mae was drawn to it. She caressed her fingertips over the smooth, sleek finish and sighed. To the left of the Southbend was a four-foot refrigerated sandwich unit. On the next wall, a window over my grandmother's ceramic sink looked out at the chicken coop and rhubarb patch. This sink would be my prep sink. In the center of the kitchen was a huge, eight-foot butcher-block table. I had the table custom-made. On the far side of the table, the builder had created a lipped edge and room for six barstools. Patrons could sit at those seats and watch the chef cook. Under the table was a small freezer/refrigerator side-by-side unit. Maximizing every single square inch of space was critical. This wasn't a mansion; it was a farmhouse. On the left-hand wall where my grandmother's sewing machine had sat for years was a three-bay sink, as well as an additional hand sink. Mae was in love. I could tell.

"The open kitchen design is important to me," I explained as her eyes drank in the beautiful space.

"This is gorgeous!" Mae praised me.

"This way."

I led us past the bar stools to the adjacent dining room. A set of French doors connected the outside deck. In the center of the room was a magnificent family-style, traditional farmhouse table. It matched the wooden top of the butcher-block island. Smooth, lightly finished chairs were tucked up close to the massive table. A red, woven runner streamed down the center. The back wall of the room was entirely windows, letting in the vivid green scenery of the fields outside.

Continuing through the large doorway to the left, we stepped into what used to be the living room. I proudly showed Mae our more private dining area. Intimate tables were pushed up against the walls. Two-tops, perfect for romantic dinners and quiet conversation. The old flat rug I remembered as a child had been ripped up and replaced by chic, dark, hardwood flooring. Lustrous red drapes scaled the windows. Tucked away in the left corner of the room under the mantle sat a red porcelain pellet stove. Two wooden rocking chairs were positioned in front of the glass door. I could hardly wait for cold winter evenings in this room as guests watched the fire jump behind the glass as heat poured from the picturesque unit. It was one of my favorite purchases so far.

Off the dining room, a half door led to a small desk and counter directly before the main entrance. This would be our front desk and host stand, where we'd welcome guests to our lovely little corner of the world before showing them to their room upstairs. I gave Mae a tour of each bedroom, complete with en-suite baths. This would be a perfect place to rest and rejuvenate.

"Amelia, I am so excited for you! This place is amazing!" Mae cheered.

We made our way back to the kitchen and sat down at the center island. I wasn't quite sure how I wanted to handle breakfast yet. It was one of the reasons I'd searched Mae out. I needed her expertise.

"So, this is what I'm imagining," I explained to my new friend. "I know you have your restaurant to think about, but is there any chance you'd want to be my pastry supplier? I'm looking for fresh-baked morning pastries to accompany breakfast, as well as a constant supply of homemade cookies for the giant cookie jar."

I pointed to the corner shelf behind the dining room table where a red, pot-bellied cookie jar sat proudly. There was never a moment that this house didn't have cookies in the cookie jar. It was a tradition I was excited to perpetuate.

"Also, I'll need desserts to offer after the evening meal. I'm open to ideas too! I want it to work best for both of us. I've often envisioned a small cheesecake bar set up somewhere..."

I looked around at the space I'd so lovingly created. Tears threatened to spill down my cheeks. I cleared my throat and stood up to get us both a glass of water. As I gazed out the window, I saw William weeding the garden.

"Hey," I turned back to Mae. "Have you lived here long? I've never heard your story."

"Oh yes," Mae nodded. "I grew up here. Some of us get stuck here, you know? This place sort of sucks us in."

In a way, I was immediately jealous of her. She had roots. But then again, if I didn't have roots, what the hell was all of this about?

"I grew up here too," I smiled. "I don't remember you, though."

"I turned thirty a few weeks ago," she added.

Ahh! I wouldn't have known Mae. Our circles wouldn't have overlapped.

"I remember hearing stories," she paused to swallow before continuing. "Stories about what happened here. Stories of the accident. I don't mean to bring it up, I just want to say I'm sorry. I can't imagine what that must have been like. And I'm glad you came home. You must be a very strong woman!"

"Some days I think I am," I smiled at her. "But most days, I think I'm downright crazy!"

I thanked her for her kind words, and we carried on our chat about cooking, baking, and scheduling. For the first time, I felt like I had a real friend and partner here. I felt happy. A little while later, as I walked Mae to her car, I noticed William was nowhere to be seen, but my gardening chores were done. I stood and watched her pull out of the driveway. I was excited about the future. Mae and I would work wonderfully together. When I turned around to walk back inside, William was standing directly behind me.

"Who was that?" he asked gruffly. His arms were folded stiffly across his flannelled chest.

I stared up at him.

"Fine, thanks, and how are you?" I replied snippily.

He didn't respond, didn't crack a smile, didn't speak.

"That's a lady who might help me in the kitchen." I rolled my eyes.

"Wonderful." His eye roll matched mine.

His sarcasm was not lost on me. He spun around to walk away, but I was faster than him. I blocked his path and stood with both hands on my hips.

"What is the problem?" I hissed angrily.

"No problem," he insisted.

"Bullshit!" I yelled.

"I don't want all these people here!" he yelled back.

"Not that," I retorted. "I don't care about that. What is your problem with me?"

My eyes softened of their own accord, against my will.

"Amelia..." he whispered as he unfolded his arms.

"What?" I whispered back. "What is it?"

"I just..." he started to explain, but I couldn't listen.

I couldn't keep my hands off him for one second longer. I quickly pushed him back against the red siding of the garage, my body pressed heavily against his.

"Tell me you don't want me, William. Tell me, and I'll leave you alone." I promised before my lips met his in a passionate suckle.

He didn't push me away. He didn't fight back. To my surprise, he swept me up into his arms and carried me up to his apartment, where he made love to me for the rest of the afternoon. He didn't hide his scars as he let me undress him. He didn't care about any of that, and I wasn't focused on his mangled shoulder. I'd forgotten what it was like to be so entranced by another. To need their touch, to surrender to it. William's big, strong hands grasped my body, and I moaned in pleasure. His walls and mine clambered to the ground around us, unmissed. To give in to each other was a sweet release, neither of us stopping to think about what might happen after. I lost myself in William, remembering his kind eyes from when I was a scared child.

His kind blue eyes had glimmered with sadness as my world fell apart.

It was at that moment I remembered William's eyes now are almost black.

Chapter 13

Days went by and I managed to avoid William. His eyes kept flashing before me in my mind, then blue, now black. Could eyes change color over the years? Was that humanly possible? If one saw enough dark things in life, could it change the shade of a pupil? Did it matter? I knew it did. I needed to figure out what was going on.

The town was withholding my liquor license. Andover had been a dry town for as long as I could remember. Alcohol could not be consumed in public. It could be purchased to take home at the local convenience store, but only after 9 am and always bagged. I had to complete a petition for the town to consider letting me serve just beer and wine. I had to canvas the community, explaining to local citizens what I was doing, and collecting signatures of people who thought it would be nice to have a lovely glass of wine with their ribeye steak at dinner. The signature part had been easy. Of course, I had to do it twice because the trusty town office ladies lost the first edition. I didn't cause a scene; I simply recollected signatures, this time getting twice the amount I had the first time. When they lost them a second time, I had my lawyer call and gently remind them of their duties as town officials. Magically, the papers reappeared, and I hadn't had much of an issue since then.

Now, I was awaiting the special town meeting where I had to convince people I was not the devil, and that the little town would not burst into flames if alcohol were consumed with meals in public. I was eager for the meeting, mostly excited to have something else to think about; something else to focus on. As I dressed to impress in my black slacks and maroon top, I missed Chloe. She was always my sounding board; the person I'd rehearse big speeches with. She usually picked out my clothes for me for things like this. I picked up my phone to FaceTime her and thought better of it. I knew what she'd say: I looked stiff, unapproachable even. I wiggled out of my black dress pants and grabbed a knee-length, flowy denim skirt. I slipped it on and stepped into my pale eggshell cowboy boots. This was Andover after all, not Portland.

The meeting went much better than expected. Occasionally, meetings in a small town can resemble a pit of angry snakes. Thankfully, this was not the case. After the votes were tallied in my favor, I lingered at the exit to thank everyone. Some people scurried by me, and I knew they voted no. Other people shook my hand and welcomed me back to the area, promising to stop in for dinner and a glass of wine as soon as we opened. I'd wondered if I should be open to the public or have meals for my guests only. Now I knew my answer. It was important to be open to the locals, if possible. They are the rafts that keep you afloat all year long, at least in theory.

The second to last person to leave was a little old lady named Thelma. She shook my hand, clasping the top of mine with her left one. Thelma had been good friends with my grandmother back in the day. I hugged her, surprised to see she was still alive. She had to be pushing ninety years old by now.

"So good to see you, dear," Thelma tweeted in my ear.

"You, too!" I smiled.

"Watch out for that man," she added briskly. "Make sure you know who you're in bed with."

She shuffled away, leaving me baffled with a sinking feeling that I should heed her advice. Small towns are notorious for everyone knowing everything; whether the knowledge is true or not is often irrelevant. The rumor mill in a small village like Andover could keep a cargo ship afloat. There are occasional times when it's nice that everyone knows everything, but more often than not, it makes your skin crawl. It makes you wish you were a stranger.

When I got home that night, to my surprise, William was waiting for me on my porch swing.

He had a bottle of red wine and a bouquet of fresh flowers.

"Hello," he said softly as I walked up the steps.

"Hello." I resisted the urge to stuff my hands in my pockets, a sure sign of insecurity. My heart raced; my palms and thighs became instantly sticky.

"I thought you might want to celebrate." He held up two stemmed glasses.

"How do you know it went well?" I couldn't remember seeing him at the meeting, but news traveled at warp speed here.

"How could anyone say no to you?"

His tone was rich and buttery. I took a couple of steps closer to him and he stood. He set the glasses down on my patio table and picked up the wine, which he'd already opened so it could breathe. He filled each glass, passed me mine, and held his glass up for a toast. I followed suit, unable to take my blue eyes away from his dark ones.

"To Lone Mountain," he proclaimed.

"To Lone Mountain," I all but whispered back.

I don't think either of us tasted the wine. Soon I was in his arms again, utterly entranced by his aura. His strong musky scent wafted in the air around me, and I was putty in his calloused hands. He carried me into the house and laid me down on the couch. His fingers explored my skin. Up and down my legs, and over my arms and shoulders until they nestled in my hair. He gripped my head and neck, massaging my scalp with his fervent fingertips. Only the moonlight streamed through the windows, and I couldn't care less what color his eyes were.

As I sat with him later that evening, darkness swallowed us on the porch swing. All too soon, it'd be too cold to sit outside at night. As it was, the soft fleece blanket draped around my body barely kept me from shivering. We'd been too lazy to start a fire. The crickets chirped around us. The air smelled of freshly cut hay, a smell I couldn't get enough of. I thought about asking William why Thelma would warn me in such a crude fashion. I thought of confiding in him about my eye color confusion, but the last thing I wanted was for him to see me like the little girl I was all those years ago. I didn't want him to think I needed rescuing all over again. I knew what I was doing now. I wasn't the same scared, shy little girl I used to be. There was no use in pretending otherwise. Besides, William was growing on me, and I was fairly certain I was growing on him. We needed each other; of that, I was positive.

***

Through harvest and into the busy hunting season, William and I saw each other as much as possible. He all but moved into my house, never officially packing and unpacking, but always falling asleep with me. I reveled in my life with him; pinching myself sometimes to be sure I wasn't dreaming. William was caring and kind, always attentive. Once in a while, he'd snap. I'd watch him unravel strand by strand. I knew he had demons deep down inside. But who didn't? He never talked about his past. He never mentioned his wounds and scars. I refused to be rude and inquire, even though I was immensely curious. When the time was right, I was sure he'd share anything he wanted me to know.

Mid-November brought cold nights and short, crisp days. William shot a deer the week before, so I was surprised when I saw him coming out of the woods with yet another dead buck. This one was smaller than the first, with only three small spikes protruding from its head. When William saw me, he looked surprised. I'd told him I was going to Portland for an overnight girls' trip. It was a long overdue jaunt into the city for a few supplies that I simply could not find around here.

"You're back." He smiled at me; his hands covered in deer blood.

"I changed my mind," I said, my voice muffled. "What's this? Didn't you already get your deer?"

"I have two permits," he replied.

"Isn't that only for one buck and one doe?" I asked. My understanding of the law was fairly evident.

"Oh, it's fine!" He bristled. "Trust me, you won't care about the gender of this creature when you're eating deer steak all winter." He laughed.

I didn't find him amusing. Here I was, going through hell trying to get all my permits and licenses perfectly correct, and William was practically illegally poaching on my property. What's worse–he was my employee. He stuck to his guns about being employed by the estate, but I owned the estate now and I hadn't once signed a paycheck for William, nor did I ever see him cash a check or go to the mailbox. Perhaps he got paid online, but as far as I knew, he didn't even own a cellphone. I couldn't picture him being the master of online banking. I'd been leaving him a little cash each week in an envelope hanging on a clipboard next to our whiteboard in the garage. The envelope always disappeared, so I assumed he needed the money.

Now, he bent to kiss my cheek and hurried off to the tool shed to hang his recent kill. I watched him go, knowing deep in my gut that Thelma was right.

Chapter 14

The next day, I sat on the sprawling hill overlooking the farm and fields. My house across the street seemed very far away, and I knew my home was never on that side of the road. It was always here, with the earth under my feet and dirt under my nails. It was in the calf barn, milk room, and on the tractor, watching and learning from my dad, not sweeping, doing dishes, laundry, and baking cookies while fighting with my sisters. Granted, all the cooking and baking made me into who I am today and left me feeling confident and knowledgeable in the kitchen. I am happy beyond measure to be doing what I love on the property I grew up on... at home.

I watched the little duck pond in the middle of the field below. Wild turkeys trudged along the bankside before scurrying away into the woods to the right. One turkey lingered behind; its entire family disappeared into the brush of the tree line. The young turkey didn't care that it was alone, not following anyone else. It happily played at the water's edge, searching for bugs and worms. I felt a kindred spirit to that turkey, alone, yet happy. Just then, to my horror, a gunshot rang out, and the turkey dropped. Dead. Just like that: happy one minute, dead the next. I watched as William walked to it, picked it up by its ankles, and dragged it back to the barn.

Tears rolled down my face. Tears for the turkey that would no doubt taste delicious at our Thanksgiving table next week, and tears for something else I couldn't quite explain. It was a feeling; dreaded knowledge that something awful was about to happen, something I would never have dared guess but feared I already knew.

***

Thanksgiving morning was bright and beautiful. Cold, but the temperature was irrelevant as I snuggled under my warm blankets with William. My hand was tracing his scars. He let me touch them without saying a word. There were so many questions I needed answered. So many thoughts I didn't speak. I couldn't. No matter how hard I tried, I couldn't form the sentences. The fact of the matter was each night I dreamt of blue eyes and each morning I woke to black ones. What did that mean?

"Hey," I said to William as he dressed. "I'd like to invite my friend Mae to dinner this afternoon. Is that okay with you?"

He paused, stretching.

"Of course." He leaned down to kiss me. "There will be plenty of food!"

"I love you," I whispered the sacred words.

He repeated them back to me. I'd recently crossed the boundary in an attempt to cleanse and reset myself; in an attempt to not hold back. I thought it would either scare William back into his shell or catapult us forward. It had done the latter. Truthfully, our relationship was flourishing. It was my best one to date. Even Chloe seemed excited for me. She wasn't coming home for Thanksgiving, but I was sure she would for Christmas. I knew this would happen once she flew the nest. California is awesome, way cooler than Mom and Maine. I understood my place, and I didn't mind because William and the farm filled my days. We were planning a Christmas opening, and I couldn't be more excited. William would be thrilled when he found all the boxes of Christmas lights I bought. This place would look like a greeting card by the time we were done decorating.

William dressed the turkey and put it in the oven before he went to the barn to do chores. I silently vowed not to eat any of it. I'd watched that happy turkey die, just so I could eat it and feel guilty. I'd bonded with that turkey. Silly, I know, for a woman whose whole business model is based on the farm-to-table idea. Either way, I would fill up on mashed potatoes, green bean casserole, and dinner rolls. I loved Thanksgiving. I was especially grateful for it this year, in this place.

I waited until William left before I slipped my feet into my cozy slippers, tossed my dark purple robe over my shoulders, and headed to the kitchen. I poured myself a cup of coffee and sat at the kitchen table with my phone. I texted Mae to invite her to our Thanksgiving meal at 2 PM. She happily agreed and said she'd bring a pie. I yawned, looking out my window toward the river. Fog rose from the direction of the riverbank as the sun attempted to heat the frosty ground. I finished my coffee and poured a second cup as I started about my busy day.

I upgraded my appliances when I moved here. Everything was stainless steel with butcher-block surfaces. I looked like a professional because I was one and I'd discovered that surrounding myself with professional things, especially in the kitchen, felt good. So that's what I did. I was quickly coming to the end of my resources, but I was confident that once we opened, I'd build my funds back up. My website and reservation systems were completed, and reservations were almost full for our opening Christmas weekend. Now we needed snow. As I thought the words, I looked out my kitchen window over my sink to see white flecks dancing in the sky. I smiled and took a deep breath as fulfillment blanketed me with a sense of security.

In Maine, so much of the tourism is dependent on the weather. Skiers and snowmobilers need snow to enjoy their coveted winter activities. They were my target market from December to March; crucial months because of the heating price tag accompanying them. We were creating an extensive cross-country skiing trail system in the woods behind the farm at the base of Lone Mountain. Cross-country skiing is one of the things I remember loving the most in my time here as a happy child, in the time before my family vanished. The farm abutted trail systems for snowmobiling and ATVs. I had maps and discounted memberships awaiting my guests. I had thermoses to fill with hot chocolate, and I'd built a sauna which would be a wonderful retreat after a cold day on the trails. I was ready, so ready to embark on this new, profound chapter.

Then Mae met William, and all my carefully crafted plans threatened to burst into flames.

CHAPTER 15

William was mashing potatoes when Mae arrived. I opened the door and ushered her inside my house, kissing her cheeks in the old movie-star way. I was feeling pretty good. William had made us pitchers of sangria, which had been flowing quite smoothly for a few hours now. Maybe I was more nervous than I realized.

"I'm so glad you could make it!" I said happily.

"Thank you for the invitation!" Mae chimed back.

"Mae, allow me to introduce you to my boyfriend." The word 'boyfriend' felt strange coming out of my mouth, but William beamed at the title. "Mae, this is William. William, this is my friend, Mae."

Mae caught her breath for a brief second before clearing her throat and holding her hand out for William to shake.

"Nice to meet you. Glad you could join us," William greeted her warmly.

"Nice to meet you," she replied. Her voice sounded odd to me.

"Here." William handed her a glass of sangria. "Please, make yourself at home. Dinner will be ready shortly."

"Thank you." She seemed to be scanning his face, his expression meeting hers blankly.

"Are you alright?" I asked under my breath.

"Oh, yes, yes I'm good! I'm great!" She shook her head as if to clear it.

I led the way into the living room, leaving William alone with the mashed potatoes. Timers would start dinging soon, but William could handle it. He had set the timers, after all. Not me. I never used a timer. Mae still seemed uneasy, and I needed to know why. We sat on the couch, both guzzling our drinks. The thought of sipping felt extremely inadequate.

"This house is beautiful! I've always wondered what it looked like in here." Mae talked as though she were trying to distract her thoughts.

"What was that back there? Are you sure you're ok? You acted like maybe you saw a ghost or something," I pried. "

"Oh, no, I'm fine!" She lied to me. I eyed her skeptically. "I just..." she started.

"Amelia, do you mind helping me with the gravy?" William asked from the kitchen.

"You just what?" I whispered to her.

"It's nothing," she replied, smiling. "Come on, gravy is the best part!" She pulled me up off the couch and I followed her into the kitchen.

Dinner was delicious. I drank so much sangria that I forgot all about the poor turkey. It was scrumptious, smothered in my rich gravy. After we cleared the table, we moved into the living room to the more comfortable chairs where we kept chatting light-heartedly. Whatever had been bothering Mae seemed to have lifted.

"Did you grow up here too?" I heard Mae ask William.

I turned to look at him as he answered yes. He didn't offer any additional information. It was about the extent of what I had been given for personal information. William liked to remain a mystery. He believed in living in the moment, now, not in the past. He told me that one night when I'd been persistently trying to get him to open up to me. I respected his outlook. I agreed with him. I felt the same way.

"You grew up here, right?" I asked Mae, even though I knew she had. We'd talked about it before.

"Yes, up in North Andover," she clarified.

I always found it comical when people said north, south, east, or west. Andover wasn't big enough to have directions.

"Were you an only child?" I asked, casually keeping the conversation going.

"No," she swallowed the last of her sangria. "I..." She cleared her throat. "I had an older brother."

"Had?" I needled her, my skin prickling.

"Yes, he...uh...he died." She refilled her glass as she spoke.

"Mae, I'm sorry. I didn't know," I apologized.

"It's okay," she shrugged. "People say he disappeared, but I know that's not true. He's dead."

I looked at William. He seemed uneasy in his recliner. His Adam's apple bobbed up and down in his throat. I waited for him to say something, but he didn't speak.

"How do you... how do you know?" I stuttered.

"I was ten when he... when he 'disappeared'." She used italics over the word and rolled her eyes as she spoke. "William was older than me, but we were best friends. He never would have just left me. I know in my gut he's dead, even if no one else will say it."

"I'm sorry, did you say William?" I asked, sitting up straighter in my seat next to her.

"Yes," she chuckled a little uneasily. "My brother's name was William. I'm sorry, that's why I was a bit flustered to meet you," she confessed to William.

"They never found a body?" I heard myself ask.

"No," Mae shook her head sadly.

"How have I never heard about this?" I said, astonished. Secrets were nearly impossible to keep here.

"We're a private family." She shrugged again. "He was so much older than me. Everyone assumes he left town for bigger and better things. I know that's not true."

"Damn." I let out a long sigh.

"But it's Thanksgiving today!" Mae rallied. "And I'm so thankful to be here with you guys! Really! Thank you! The holidays can be so lonely."

"Well, not anymore!" I winked at her. "You can always be here with us."

I reached over to squeeze William's hand. It was ice cold. I couldn't look at him. Instead, I looked into Mae's brilliant blue eyes and smiled sadly.

That night I dreamed of black eyes. Eyes that pulled Alice out of the doorway that fateful day. Eyes that made my mother angry with rage. Eyes that sucked the life out of my sisters. I woke in a sweat; beads of perspiration dripping from my face to my pillowcase. I looked at the man who was sleeping soundly beside me. The man I'd come to love, the man who chilled at Mae's story this evening. I stood and went to the kitchen for a glass of water.

I refused to believe I was sleeping with Xander. I wouldn't allow myself to even contemplate the thought. It was impossible. But the scars... the silent scars told a story that lips would never mutter. I had come to not only need William, but to appreciate him. He was sincere and kind. He took initiative in more ways than one. He made me feel special. There was no way he was Xander; no way he was the mean, spiteful, rude boy who had shattered my family. But his eyes...

I drove myself crazy not trying to connect the dots. The bold dots that were mounted with red flags. I needed William. I needed him on the farm. I needed him to do chores while I fed guests their farm fresh breakfasts. I needed him to hay and plow and feed cattle. I needed him to be my partner. He felt like my partner. He loved this place. This land was his home, too. Xander would never feel that way.

I drank my water and went back to bed. Surely it was a fluke thing. William was a common name, after all.

Chapter 16

The next day, Mae stopped by unannounced to apologize for her sour storytelling the day before.

"Oh girl, please don't apologize." I hugged her.

"Holidays make me a little crazy," she admitted meekly. "It's hard with the family all gone. I'm sure you know." She touched my arm gently.

"I do know," I assured her. "And you don't need to be sorry, honestly. I value your friendship and want to know everything there is to know about you!"

"Do you want to go for a walk?" she asked.

"Sure!" I nodded. "I'd love to. Let me grab us some orange."

I hurried to the garage. Mae had caught me on my way to the farmhouse from the hay barn, where

William and I had enjoyed a little post-Thanksgiving bliss. Now he was building new stalls in the barn, and I was deep in thought per usual. Mae and I adorned ourselves in hunter orange and started off to walk the back acres of the property where the stream from the mountain grew into a babbling brook. As we walked, I felt Mae ease a bit, as did I. It'd been so long since I had a real friendship, I'd almost forgotten how they work. The authentic, mystical friendships where you can tell each other anything, have uncomfortable conversations and still be friends afterward. I felt like that was what I was building with Mae, but I wasn't confident enough to test it. Not yet.

As we walked, she told me she was on vacation until mid-December.

"It gets so quiet here," she said. "Until the snow flies, at least."

We had taken a right at the old tool shed. A shed William had fortified with new posts and beams, and a new roof to ensure its survival. As we walked along, we talked about how much we were praying for snow for the upcoming season. We jumped across the rippling brook, skipping on the few flat rocks that kept us dry as we went.

"Nothing's frozen here yet," Mae commented as we hiked up the slight bank, leaving the water behind. "The ground isn't even close to frozen." She kicked at the soil. The dirt shifted, and a bone protruded from the earth.

"It's been a long time since I've been way out here," I reminisced, looking up at the sky. "The trees seemed taller when I was a child."

"Um, Amelia," Mae called out to me. "That's a bone."

"Oh," I said disinterestedly. "Yeah, my dad used to bury dead livestock out here. Beef carcasses, you know, got to love that circle of life," I joked. "He used to tap trees out here, too. We'll do that this spring. Mmm, I can't wait for our real maple syrup."

"Amelia, this is a human skull!" Mae yelled from deeper into the woods, where she'd wandered off, following the bones.

"What?" I scoffed and ran to where she was scrunched down at the base of a big pine tree.

"Fuck!" I whispered to my new friend.

This can't be real, I thought. But sure enough, bones littered the surrounding ground. Human bones. I bent and picked up a small, straight bone. A finger, maybe. I shivered.

"What are you ladies up to?" William's voice sounded from the edge of the trees.

I quickly slipped the bone up into the wristband of my orange sweatshirt.

"Just exploring," I announced as we walked out to where he was standing at the edge of the trees. "I'm showing Mae the property and all my crazy ideas." I tried to sound normal, keeping my body language as soft as possible. I leaned in and kissed my boyfriend, whoever he may be. "I was telling her we're going to tap these trees come spring."

"Oh, we are, are we?" He wrapped his arms around me playfully.

I smiled up at him. I'd somehow managed to break through William's facade over these last few months. I'd uncovered a sweet, lonely cowboy. He wasn't anyone who would harm another person. William had his secrets, as did everyone. But he certainly wasn't Xander, right? And what of these bones? Could the bone rubbing against my wrist right now be Mae's brother's? Was their shared name a coincidence? Did I believe in coincidence?

Know who you're in bed with... Thelma's warning rang out loudly in my mind, a bell that kept tolling louder and louder and louder. I couldn't confront William without proof. We needed to test these bones. I needed to know who this dead body belonged to. I would never rest otherwise. Beyond that, could I open my business in exactly one month, when human bones were scattered around the property? What if it wasn't William's body? Who else could it be?

"I'm going to order a pizza for lunch. Do you want to come into town and get it with us?" I asked William.

The silence that had unfolded around us was stressing me out. Probably jumping from dead body to pizza surprised Mae, but she followed my lead.

"Ooh, thin crust is my favorite," she inserted her two cents.

I knew William wouldn't go with us. He never went past the dump road. Again, another brightly illuminated red flag, which I chose to ignore. I didn't say a word as I took out my cell phone and called the corner store. I placed an order for a pepperoni, pineapple, and jalapeno pizza with thin crust and extra cheese.

"Twenty minutes," I said, clicking my phone shut. "Should we head back?"

I didn't wait for a response from anyone. I grasped William's hand in mine as we started the stroll back to the farm. Mae was quiet. She walked next to me. I looked at her, praying she could read my expression, begging her to be calm. We both seemed to know we were walking with a murderer, buying our time with worthless chatter.

When we got back to Mae's car, I kissed William goodbye, and we drove uptown. We parked in front of the run-down old store. Everything in Andover needed a fresh coat of paint. Neither one of us spoke until finally I reached into the wrist of my sleeve and removed the bone. Shaking, I handed it to Mae, but she wouldn't take it.

"My William is dead," she said softly. "I don't need these bones to tell me that's true. Those results will affect your life a lot more than mine."

I knew what she was trying to do, and I appreciated her for it. She didn't want to flip my life upside down. She didn't want to mess up my opening and all my hard work. Another dead body on my property would certainly distract visitors. But could I live like that? Not knowing? I knew it would eat me alive. Mae had made peace with her past, but I knew I couldn't move forward with my future until I figured this out. We got our pizza and then drove to the library on Church Street next to my preschool teacher's house. For a moment, I wondered if she still lived there, but I quickly reminded myself to stay on course. I went in, leaving Mae in the car, and used the computer to order a DNA test. I printed off the label, thanked the nice librarian, and got back in the car. Mae knew what I was doing, and I think she was grateful. We drove a few feet to the post office where I went in, purchased a padded envelope, and secured the mystery bone inside with my self-adhesive label. I paid the attendant, giving her my package, which I mailed overnight express before I returned to the car.

"I won't tell you the results if you don't want to know," I promised.

"Oh, I want to know." She raised her eyebrows.

"I need to know." I blew out a deep breath. "Because if those remains are your brother's, there's a very good chance my William is a fraud. There's a very good chance I'm sleeping with my sisters' killer.

"But how?" she inquired as we slowly drove home with our pizza.

"There's always been something a bit odd about him," I admitted. "Red flags I've pretended not to see. Did your...did your brother ever work on the farm? Do you remember?" I asked the question I'd been dying to ask since I learned of Mae's brother.

"I'm not sure," she replied. "He was so much older than me."

"Did he... did he have blue eyes?" I whispered.

"The kindest blue eyes you've ever seen." Mae's eyes glistened at the recollection.

"Fuck," I said, shaking my head. "I should have bought a condo in Myrtle Beach."

CHAPTER 17

There have been many times in my life when I've had well-thought-out, carefully executed plans. Coming home after all these years has been my most well-planned mission yet... until now. Now I had no clue what to do. I had so many strands all braided together, each one relying on the next. And William, well, he had somehow become the ripcord, threatening to ruin everything without provocation. He didn't know I knew the truth. He didn't know I knew he was the person I loathed the most in this world. And I couldn't tell him I knew.

Mae stopped coming around and I couldn't blame her. I couldn't look her in the eyes. I felt dirty for sleeping with her brother's killer, and my sisters', really my mother's and father's too. I was the only survivor of that day, me and the truck driver. Suddenly, I stopped. The egg in my hand fell to the countertop, breaking on the wooden surface instead of in the bowl of muffin batter. We had finally opened two weeks ago. Our Christmas grand opening went better than I ever could have imagined, followed by a terrific New Year's weekend. Several community members stopped in with flowers and congratulatory messages. Everyone was amazed at what I'd done with the place. William stayed out of sight; his chores were always done, but he was never visible to others. In my mind, this only solidified his guilt, but I dared not broach the subject with him. At night, when I walked home after a long day of hosting guests on the farm, he was always there to comfort me, yet I took no comfort in his touch anymore. He didn't seem to notice. I was a decent faker, a quality I hated about myself. I longed to yell at him, to punch him, to tear at his scars with all my might. Instead, I did nothing.

I cleaned the broken egg off my counter, the slippery gooiness fought against my paper towel, clinging to the surface of my workspace. My mind raced like a car flipped over, the wheels still spinning uncontrollably. Why had I never thought about the truck driver until now? I racked my brain trying to remember the man's name. The logging industry was a vital part of our area. Andover was home to countless loggers, some independent, others working for larger companies. Sustainable forestry kept many families here alive, except for mine.

All day, I thought about who the mystery driver was, but it must not have been a fact I dwelled on at ten years old because I couldn't remember. Finally, at my scheduled break at 3 PM, when my guests were all otherwise occupied, I slipped into my office and sat down at my grandfather's roll-top desk. I dug out the old hard copy phonebook that I'd found collecting dust. There was only one person who could help me, and I hoped her memory was still intact enough to do so. I thumbed through the pages, finally landing on the R's. Randelle... Reed... Ritman... Ritter. Ritter! There it was: Thelma Ritter. I dialed the number, praying she still had a landline.

207-392-4071.

"Hello?" The little old lady on the other end answered on the third ring.

"Hello, Mrs. Ritter, it's me." I cleared my throat. "It's Amelia. Amelia Brackley from Lone Mountain. I was just..." I stopped and sighed heavily into the receiver.

"Speak up, dear! I can't hear you!" Thelma squawked.

"Thelma, do you remember the accident when Jenny and Alice were killed? Do you remember who the truck driver was?" I hollered.

"Of course I do. It was my Alvin," she snapped back.

"Your Alvin?" I repeated. "Your... your?"

"My husband. He had his own small logging operation back in the day," she elaborated.

"Oh!" I sat up straighter in my wheeled office chair. Maybe this would be easier than I thought. "Ma'am, is he home? Could I speak to him? I'm trying to do some research about that day."

"No, you cannot speak to him," she cackled.

"Please, it'll only take a moment," I begged.

"He's dead!" Her voice bellowed into my ear.

"Oh," was the only thing I could think to say.

"He took his own life, not a week after the accident." Her tone softened a bit.

"I'm...I'm so sorry. I didn't know," I said, shocked. How had I not known this? What else didn't I know?

"What are you researching, dear? My memory is about the only thing that still works," she laughed a little then.

"I... I don't want to bother you," I said, my heart still in my throat over this recent news.

"If it's about that boy..." She let her voice trail off.

"I know all about that," I admitted quietly.

"No one ever thought he was capable of killing like that," Thelma acknowledged. "If my Alvin had been alive, he would have..."

"Wait? What? Who?" I was confused.

"You'd gone off to college by then, dear. You weren't around when that boy returned to apologize. I was there when it happened. I was having tea with your grandmother." Thelma's voice was accusatory.

"Which boy?" My head was spinning, filtering through her unnecessary tone. Didn't she know I felt bad enough already?

"That boy that killed your sisters." She sounded muffled now, like she was very far away.

Did she even know what she was talking about? How old was she now? Ninety? So Xander did come back? That settled it, I guess.

"William had come back home that summer to help your grandfather with the farm," Thelma explained. "He answered the door when that boy knocked."

"Xander came back to apologize?" I asked for clarification, my heart leaping in my throat, unbidden.

"Xander, yes! That was his name!" Thelma said excitedly.

I could picture the encounter in my mind, William answering the door to find Xander standing on the other side.

"What... what happened?" I stammered.

"William took one look at him in the doorway and strangled him to death with his bare hands."

I was mute. Only static could be heard on the line. Finally, I swallowed hard and spoke.

"William killed Xander?" I asked, bewildered.

"You'd know this dear, if you'd ever come home to visit!" Thelma chastised me.

She was right. I'd left for college and never returned, not even for my grandparent's funerals years later. I couldn't. My grief was too unsettling. It was only through the years with Chloe that I managed to overcome my pain and guilt. So much guilt.

"Thelma," I fought back the engorged lump in my throat. "What happened to William?"

"Oh, he left, by golly, after he and your grandfather buried Xander's body deep in the back forty, where no one would ever find it."

I immediately thought of the bones Mae and I found. Thankfully, they were now buried under snow. We received a foot of heavy powder a week before Christmas, much to my delight.

"He just left?" I asked my informant.

"He probably killed himself too, would be my guess," Thelma said matter-of-factly. "Death eats away at a person, you know?"

"I do." I breathed heavily.

Silence ensued for a full minute before I was able to form the next question.

"Thelma, if he's not William, and he's not Xander, then who is the man in my bed?" I spoke slowly and clearly for fear that I'd have to repeat myself.

"Why, that's Xander's twin brother, William. I thought you said you knew this, dear?" She tittered the way old ladies do; her tongue sounded like it was stuck to the roof of her dentures.

"William must have been a popular name back then," I muttered.

"William is a strong, sure name, just like Alvin," she schooled me.

"Yes, ma'am," I agreed. "And how did he get to be on the farm?"

"Why, he showed up, looking for his brother. Your grandfather sat him down and had a nice long talk with him, and he's been there ever since. He never left. He saved that farm, William did. He is a good man. He wanted to make restitution for his brother's mistakes. He cared for the place after your grandparents took sick. Such a good man." I could almost feel Thelma nodding her head in approval.

"Interesting." I didn't know what else to say.

"You know, I was there when those boys were born. William's shoulder and arm were mangled from sharing the womb with that monstrous brother of his." Thelma added this little tidbit of trivia.

Images of William's shoulder and upper arm danced in my mind. He used to shrink back every time I tried to touch it. I'd all but solidified his guilt based on his disfigurement. I was sure he'd suffered those scars from the accident he caused. I couldn't have been further from the truth. And I couldn't have been happier to be so wrong.

"Why did you tell me to watch out for him?" I asked my last question.

"I didn't mean to scare you, dear," Thelma replied. "I just thought you should be aware."

"You said, 'Watch out for that man'. Why did you say that?" I pressed her further, thinking about all the sleepless nights I'd endured while my mind spiraled out of control.

"Everyone has demons, dear. I meant watch out for him, like take care of him."

I thought of William's dark eyes, his far-away expressions, and his broodiness. Certainly, everyone did have demons. I wasn't free of them myself.

"Thelma, thank you for talking with me, and I'm very, very sorry about Alvin," I said warmly before hanging up the phone.

Thoughts of William raced a million miles a minute in my mind. Of course, he'd been weird at Thanksgiving with Mae! Her brother killed his brother! Now the only worry I had was that foolish bone that I'd sent off to the lab. Did random bones get sent off to DNA facilities all the time? Was it a regular occurrence? Surely, my envelope couldn't be the only one with someone's finger in it. For all they knew, it was someone's finger lost in a sawmill accident. That was known to happen here in the Maine woods. Would they analyze the bone and send it back to the sender like they did with toothbrushes and hair embedded in sweater fabrics? *'Thank you for the bone and your $150 fee. Here are your results and returned property.'* Is that how it would go? I slumped over onto my grandfather's desk, unsure of what to do with this mess I'd created.

Chapter 18

I unchained myself from my chair; the weights around my ankles were nonexistent yet heavier than anything I'd ever felt before. I could barely move, stunned by the recent revelation of my phone call with Thelma. I slowly trudged toward the employee entrance, unsure of how I wanted to talk to William, but knowing we had to have a conversation. I was in the wrong. Not him. I was the one who thought I was with someone entirely different this whole time we'd been together. While that was true, he had gone along with it. But I suppose I couldn't blame him for that. Still, I thought he should have come clean. He should have told me who he really was. Would it have mattered? Of course, it would have. His brother killed my family.

I opened the door and stepped onto the porch just as William was stepping up onto it from outside. He met me in the middle of the breezeway holding a padded yellow envelope. I knew in my gut I was about to get the answer I'd been wondering about. Four to six weeks, the website had said. He handed me the package. It read: 'DNA RESULTS ENCLOSED'. Apparently, in my haste at the library, I hadn't checked the box for privacy.

"What is this?" William asked as I took the package from him.

"Oh boy," I said, sighing. "Come sit with me and I will tell you."

We walked around to the back side of the breezeway where it was screened in. This time of year, glass covered the screens. Normally, we wouldn't sit in here during the winter months. It was too cold for that. It would be nice in the warmer months, especially when the sun hits this side of the house. For now, though, I figured the chill in the air would help me focus as I came clean to William about my recent discovery. He sat and listened in his calm, collective way.

"So, all this time, you thought I was the other William?" he asked once I'd finally finished speaking.

"No... not all the time," I admitted.

"Oh yes, for a while there, you thought I was Alexander, my brother who killed your sisters." His voice was starting to take on a hostile tone now.

"I don't... I don't know what I was thinking," I responded timidly.

"Why didn't you just ask me?" He wanted to know.

"Ask you if you were Xander? Ask you if you're lying? Based on what? A hunch?" I scoffed. "I wasn't willing to throw us away on a hunch. I needed proof."

"Well, open your proof." He pointed to the unopened envelope resting on my lap.

"I don't... I don't need to know," I lied.

"Yes, you do."

He took the package from me and opened it himself. The bone fell to his lap. He handed me the paper letter without looking at it. The big bold word in red ink at the top of the page took me by surprise. 'INCONCLUSIVE'.

"What?" I gasped, defeated.

"What does it say?" William asked.

"It says, inconclusive." I dropped the letter onto my lap.

"Those bones are old; they've been buried out there for twenty years. And where did you send this to?" He picked up the paper and read the heading out loud. "DNAworks.com? Please tell me you did not send them money. This is not professional." He eyed me.

"150 bucks!" I crumpled the paper up, refusing to make eye contact with William as I sat back on the loveseat and pouted like a child.

"Oh, baby!" He laughed at me and pulled me into his chest. I snuggled into him, feeling like a huge weight had been lifted, feeling like I was finally home.

"Listen, why don't we take this bone and go to Augusta, to the University, and let the budding young scientists analyze it? They could even take my blood for cross-reference. I'm sure they'd love to..."

"No, no, I'm good. Honest." I interrupted him. "I feel better knowing the truth, the whole story. And Thelma was right, it's my fault for staying away so long. Too long. This is my home. I should have raised my daughter here. I should have..."

"You can't live your life on 'should-haves'." William kissed my forehead. "Besides, if you hadn't left, who knows what might have happened?"

"True. I could have answered the door that night instead of William. Maybe Xander would still be alive. Maybe Mae would still have her brother."

"Maybe you and I would have never met," William finished my thought. "Life doesn't work that way. You can't go back and reroute. Alexander was evil. Even as a kid, he was mean. I used to say he had black blood to match his black eyes. He was destined for destruction. Hell, he destroyed my shoulder in vitro, I'm sure of it."

Something in me shifted, a new perspective, perhaps. I climbed onto William's lap and un-snapped the shirt under his jacket. He shivered as

I pressed my cold hands against the rippled skin of his shoulder.

"Does this hurt?" I asked softly.

"No," he replied. "It's just ugly from all the surgeries."

I bowed my head, kissing his taught flesh. His scars were a reminder that his twin brother was always with him. And I knew my sisters would always be with me, even though they were gone. Even though I never got to say goodbye. My fault or not, it didn't matter. Our stories make up our past and mold our future. They create us, maiming us along the way. That's life.

Just then the doorbell rang, bringing me back to the here and now. Back to the restful retreat I'd created with William. I had guests waiting to check-in. Guests who would relax and rejuvenate here on the farm as they explored nature and ate delicious home-grown food. I walked to the main entrance and opened the door to let in a family waiting on the other side. A mom, a dad, and three daughters.

"Hello there! Welcome to Lone Mountain! We're so glad you're here!" I greeted them warmly.

Tonight, those three sisters would learn how to milk a cow. Tomorrow morning, they'd help collect eggs. In the afternoon, there would be sledding and skating and marshmallows over an open fire. Irreplaceable memories in the making. William and I, with the curative essence of Lone Mountain, had helped heal each other somehow, and now we would give back wholeheartedly. We would make the world around us a better place. My mother would be happy, I thought, as I showed the family around the farmhouse. And my father... he'd be proud of his farm-girl daughter and the beautiful space I'd created here on the farm. Here, at home.

www.ingramcontent.com/pod-product-compliance
Lightning Source LLC
LaVergne TN
LVHW041812060526
838201LV00046B/1235